SEP 2 8 2005 CF

P9-AOD-408

STREET
MAGIC

STREET
MAGIC

MICHAEL REAVES

A TOM DOHERTY ASSOCIATES BOOK NEW YORK

This is a work of fiction. All the characters and events portrayed in this book are fictitious, and any resemblance to real people or events is purely coincidental.

STREET MAGIC

Copyright © 1991 by Michael Reaves

All rights reserved, including the right to reproduce this book, or portions thereof, in any form.

A Tor Book
Published by Tom Doherty Associates, Inc.
49 West 24th Street
New York, N.Y. 10010

Library of Congress Cataloging-in-Publication Data

Reaves, Michael.
      Street magic / Michael Reaves.
          p.   cm.
      "A Tom Doherty Associates book."
      ISBN 0-312-85125-1
      I. Title.
   PS3568.E269S7   1991
   813'.54—dc20   90-29150
                                  CIP

First edition: July 1991

Printed in the United States of America

0 9 8 7 6 5 4 3 2 1

For Brynne, and for Steve. What the hell.

ACKNOWLEDGMENTS

Grateful acknowledgment is made, in no particular order, to Paul Dini, David Stager, Richard Kadrey, John Shirley, Martha Soukup, Pat Russell, Curt Batiste, Gerry Conway, Phillip Vardara, Dena Ramras and Martha Millard. And most especially Beth Meacham, Brynne Stephens and Steve Perry, without whom this book—well, you know.

A world ends when its metaphor has died.
—*Archibald MacLeish*

PART ONE

THE CITY UNDER THE HILL

There is another shore, you know, upon the other side.
—*Lewis Carroll*

1

Danny Thayer was working his "robbin' street": Broadway just west of Columbus Avenue. It was evening, the best time for hustling the crowds that drifted beneath the neon signs advertising nude dancing and X-rated movies. Danny was alone this cool April night. Normally Roberto would be with him; it was never a good idea to hit the streets without a partner, someone to be your eyes behind. Though many of the street people were his friends, there were very few that he trusted completely; he always had to be hip to the possibility of being rolled for whatever small amount of change he had in his threadbare jeans.

Roberto, however, had spent most of the day throwing up. It was Danny's opinion that his friend's dinner had sat for a bit too long in the trash bin behind the Twin Dragon restaurant. He hoped that was all it was; he didn't like to think about the possibility of Roberto being seriously ill.

"'Scuse me, sir, can you spare some change so I can

get my sister something to eat? She's pregnant, y'know—eating for two . . ."

Sometimes they said yes; sometimes they said no. Mostly they simply walked past, looking through him as though he didn't exist. Those were the ones he hated the most. His mother had often ignored him in just that way, preferring not to see what was going on in her home.

Though he was always aware of the possibility of danger, Danny wasn't particularly nervous about being alone on the streets. He had never been taken down, though a couple of kids he had encountered in the past few months had not been so lucky. He thought about one of them: a black girl from Indianapolis named Denise. He and Roberto had done everything they could after finding her where she had been dumped in an alley not far from their squat, but they hadn't even been able to stop the bleeding. Danny's mind shied away from the memory of the bubbling sound she had made when she cried.

He had seen some of the older street people eyeing him on occasion, but they never gave him trouble. Roberto said it was because God watches over dumbshit out-of-towners, but Danny had his own theory. He figured it was because of his magic.

"Pardon me, ma'am, but I need some money to buy a bus ticket back home . . . could you spare a dollar?"

That was one that usually worked pretty well, though it was the biggest lie of the bunch; there was no way Danny would ever even think of going back to L.A. He had been in the Bay Area for almost two months now: two months of tenements and cheap motels, nine or ten to a room with other runaways, living on Preludin, hot dogs, and cheap wine, begging and raiding dumpsters to stay alive. Currently he and Roberto and Birdclaw were squatting in a condemned hotel south of Market. They had

4

moved all the furniture that wasn't completely broken down into what had been the largest suite, and they carried water up in buckets once a day from a nearby gas station.

It wasn't too bad a life, all things considered, especially with Roberto there. Roberto was four years older than Danny and had been in the army before receiving a dishonorable discharge—for what, he refused to talk about. Roberto was tall and wore studded leather armbands around his hard biceps. He shaved his head and had a Fu Manchu mustache. Danny thought that looked great; if he ever produced enough facial hair to warrant shaving, he intended to trim his that way.

Danny prowled his chosen corner restlessly, a thin sixteen-year-old boy with a blue bandanna bound around his greasy hair. He could see Tin Head shambling up the other side of the street, duffel bag slung over one shoulder. Tin Head was a shapeless figure wrapped in layers of soiled coats and wearing hip-length fishing boots. Danny and the other runaways called him Tin Head because he lined the inside of his hat with tinfoil to keep out Russian microwaves. There were a lot of people on the street who were crazy, but Tin Head was *really* crazy. He talked to Jesus in a loud voice, and often refused money when it was offered.

Perhaps half a block down on Danny's side of the street a young black man stood in front of a bar playing a saxophone. The horn's case lay open on the sidewalk in front of him. Danny had drifted down the street perhaps ten minutes previously and glanced at the musician's take. It was paltry; a couple of one-dollar bills and a handful of change. It was a slow night.

Roberto had taken care of Danny almost from the day that Danny had jumped off the freight. He had taught

5

Danny to be streetwise: how to sift the contents of a dumpster for food; where the best places to spare-change in the city were; how to tell decent dope from stuff that had been stepped on more often than the sidewalk. From him Danny had learned that it was possible to live on the streets without grabbing his ankles or getting his tonsils sticky. Roberto was very concerned about the possibility of diseases, especially AIDS. Danny felt he owed quite a bit to Roberto.

"'S'happenin'?"

Danny turned around to see Shanti, a scrawny brunette with soulful brown eyes, hugging a torn sweater around her against the chill spring of San Francisco. Shanti belonged to Duke, a pimp who was notorious for beating up his girls when they failed to bring in enough money. She had shown Danny the scars left from a whipping he had given her with a length of red-hot wire last week. This week she had pulled four tricks in an effort to please him. One of them had left her with a purplish bruise on the left side of her face, and Duke had beaten her again for letting herself get marked where it showed. Shanti had just turned fourteen.

"Nothin' much," Danny replied. "You okay?"

She gave a shrug that turned into a shiver. "Sure." Her gaze flicked nervously about the street, appraising possible johns. "Bummer night, huh?"

Danny remembered Roberto once asking Shanti why her parents had named her that. She told him her folks were ex-hippies, and that "shanti" meant "peace." Roberto had started laughing and asked her how she spelled that. Danny had not thought the joke particularly funny.

"Yeah, I only got ten bucks or so, and I been here since three." Danny could see the desperation in her eyes. She had to bring some money back tonight, he knew.

Shanti was about to say something else when she noticed something behind him. He turned in time to see a BMW turn out of the stream of traffic and pull up to the curb beside them. A tinted window slid smoothly down, and inside Danny caught a glimpse of a charcoal-gray suit behind the wheel. He thought of his father.

Shanti was already heading toward the car when he caught her arm. "Wait. I don't think you ought to go."

"I got to! Else Duke'll get really mad."

"You're gonna get hurt sometime doin' this," he said helplessly.

She shrugged again. "Whatever happens, happens." She opened the BMW's door and slid into the dark interior. Danny leaned over the window. "Here, I want you to have this." He dug something out of his pocket and dropped it in her hand.

She glanced at it. "A marble? What—?"

"It's not really a marble. It's a spellstone. I put a spell on it, to protect you. Keep you from gettin' hurt."

Shanti looked in confusion for an instant at the small glass ball in her hand, then looked back at Danny and smiled shyly. "Thanks, Danny. You're sweet."

The window rose, replacing her face with the reflection of his own. Danny watched as the BMW sped off into traffic. Shanti, he knew, looked down on dumpster diving and panhandling as a means of survival; she had said more than once that getting forty dollars a date or twenty for unzipping some horny businessman in his car was a much easier way to make money, even though she had to give most of it to Duke. Danny couldn't understand her attitude. It seemed foolish to him to do anything to earn money when the city cast out so much free food and other bounty every day. Turning dates seemed especially demeaning; it was a point of pride with him that he hadn't yet

7

been forced to that. Of course, there was Roberto—but Roberto was different. Roberto was his friend.

The other one living in the abandoned hotel was Birdclaw, an aging punk with spiked red hair. He had gotten his nickname after riding the rails too stoned to avoid an oncoming freight that had cut off the last two fingers of his right hand. Birdclaw wanted to be a rocker; he had a cheap electric guitar and was trying to put together enough bucks to buy an amp. He hung around the clubs mostly, dealing a little dope and trying to get next to some of the local bands. Roberto had told Birdclaw more than once that he sang like a canary in a blender, but Birdclaw said that hadn't stopped a lot of others who were getting paying gigs. He certainly looked the part, in Danny's opinion. And he was generous with his dope, which went a long way toward helping the others tolerate his endless screeching of his songs.

Danny sighed and shook his head. He wasn't going to fill his pockets by standing around thinking. He noticed a likely mark coming toward him: an older couple, wearing clothes that were expensive but not ostentatious. " 'Scuse me, but my dad's sick and I got to buy him some medicine. Could you—?"

DANNY REMAINED ON THE street until well past midnight. When he finally decided to go home the fog was thickening, rolling in from the bay and over the rumpled streets of San Francisco like an avalanche in slow motion. He was shivering as he hurried along; his denim jacket did little to keep out the dampness, and he had worn a hole in the canvas top of one of his boat shoes and could feel the damp air chilling his toes. He thrust his hands deeper into his pockets and stepped up his pace, heading west toward Powell.

He thought about using some of the day's take to ride a bus at least partway—it was a long walk back to the Larkspur Hotel. But the day's take had amounted to little more than twelve dollars in quarters, dimes and dollar bills in his pockets. Best to save it. Roberto was sick, after all, and Danny might have to buy some medicine for him.

He passed the wooden shelves and bright lights of an all-night newsstand and, even though it was late and he had a long way to go, he tarried. He stared at the hundreds of magazines and books, wishing, as always, that he could read better. He could make his way through a comic book with some help, but the lines of text on a printed page were often too much for him. He saw the cover of a fantasy novel turned toward the street: a band of snarling trolls stood before a chest of treasure, facing a young wizard and a buxom, scantily clad maiden. The wizard was armed with a magic wand. Danny smiled. As he turned down Powell his imagination provided a sort of double vision, as it had many times before; he was not really walking the streets of San Francisco, but rather the avenues of some nameless magical city. He picked up a broken car aerial from the gutter; he was Merlin the Magician, and this was the magic wand that would protect him while he sought the treasure of the trolls. There was great danger all about him, but while he carried his wand none could attack him. He would find the treasure and it would make him the wealthiest wizard in the kingdom . . .

Danny walked quickly down Powell, passing the box hedges and flowered paths of Union Square. The lights of the Hyatt Regency and the other tall buildings surrounding him were dim and ghostly in the fog. It was still a long way to the Larkspur Hotel, and the spring night was cold and wet. He walked faster, turning down a side street that sloped away steeply into a pool of grayness. Two eerie

9

lights rose out of the mist. Danny hid within a recessed doorway, gesturing with the wand to render himself invisible (or invincible; he could never remember which word was right).

A dragon eased up the hill, its two blazing eyes framing a gridwork of bared metallic teeth. Danny gestured defiantly with the wand as the creature passed, then started down into the luminous fog. He feared nothing, for his magic was the strongest in the kingdom. The fantasy comforted him, as it always did; the weather did not seem quite so bad now.

Even Roberto, who was undoubtedly his best friend, was not aware of the truth about him. Danny had never told him, had never told anyone, about his magic. Somehow he knew that to do so would be to lose it, and to lose his magic would be to lose his only real reason for living. The magic nestled within him, a tiny warm fire at the core of his being, protected from and protecting him from all outsiders. He would never do anything to risk it.

Because someday, he knew, his magic would take him home.

"Home" was not the big, impersonal mansion in the Pacific Palisades where he had grown up. No, home was a much better place—his own world. He called it Middle Earth, a term he had read once in a comic book. Danny's conception of Middle Earth bore little resemblance to Tolkien's realm; Minas Tirith had no place there, but New York City did, as did the Lost Boys' House and Opar. Spider-Man, the Incredible Hulk and Indiana Jones fought there side-by-side with Robin Hood, Popeye the Sailor and Tarzan. Flash Gordon and Buck Rogers pursued white rabbits and battled Godzilla, King of the Monsters. Danny spun long and intricate tales to himself about these lands and characters, as well as others borrowed from movies, rock songs and comics as he encountered them.

Over the years Danny had come to believe in his Middle Earth as more than a mental haven from reality—he knew it was real, that it existed somewhere. Sometimes he got flashes of images from it that were so real he could swear that he had already seen its legendary forests and hills, perhaps in a previous life. Danny had never really questioned any of this; he just knew that it was the case. Somewhere there was a land of always afternoon, where elves and goblins and smurfs cavorted and played, where Green Lantern rescued maidens in distress from Freddy Krueger and Ozzy Osbourne before Ozzy could bite their heads off. And Danny knew with the same certainty that someday, somehow, he would find a way to escape there. It was, at times, all that kept him going.

He could remember a time, vaguely, when life had been different at home, before the bad things started happening. He had never known what exactly had caused the difference in the way he had been treated—he felt certain, however, that it had somehow been his fault. He remembered a day just after his tenth birthday, his father pushing him in his swing set in the backyard of their house in Lawrence, Kansas. It had been a beautiful spring day and he had felt it entirely possible that his feet could almost reach the bright clouds in the clear sky. He laughed out loud from the sheer exuberance of being alive, of the strong feeling his arms had as they pulled against the chains of the swing. It seemed at that moment that if he let go at the apex of his swing, he would simply continue going, soaring up into the clouds, breaking the bonds of gravity like a superhero.

He remembered his father laughing as well and calling encouragement to him as he pushed him higher and higher. It was one of the last pleasant memories before they had moved to Los Angeles, where it had all changed . . .

His mind occupied with such thoughts, Danny turned a corner and was taken aback to find himself suddenly face to face with a small figure hidden in an oversized pea coat. He heard a gasp and raised the wand reflexively, then dropped it with a cry of pain. He stared in disbelief at his hand, at the red welt that crossed his palm, and then at the aerial, still glowing faintly on the sidewalk before him. He looked up; the stranger in the pea coat was gone. The street was empty.

"No!" he cried.

The cry of denial burst from Danny before he could stop it, even had he wanted to. In the instant it had taken to feel the searing pain of the burn, he had known, had *known,* why and how it had come to be there.

He stared, searched, reached out with everything he had—all the muddled desire and inchoate longing he had lived with for so long had focused within him in that single, wrenching cry. The stranger who had stood before him, who had vanished in the brief second his gaze had dropped, was, he knew without doubt, his ticket home.

He blinked. The fog seemed to waver for a moment. Then he saw a dim silhouette far ahead, running.

He began to run in pursuit. Stitches stabbed him under his ribs, but he kept his eyes fixed on the fleeing figure, not even daring to blink, aware somehow that if he lost whoever it was this time it would be forever.

Whoever it was, he or she was faster than Danny by far, and beginning to melt into the fog. Danny kept running. He had no breath to shout again, and no idea what he should say if he could. But he was not able to keep up his pace. The silhouette faded into the mist.

12

Danny came to a stop, limping, the cold, damp air burning his lungs. He kept staring into the grayness, hoping, knowing that it was fruitless. He began to cry quietly, scarcely realizing he was doing so. Tears ran down his thin cheeks, dampening the scarf he wore. He felt confused, lost, bewildered. His certainty did not waver, however; he knew that the mysterious figure could have rescued him. The welt on his hand still pained him. It was proof that he had been witness to magic this night.

He was not sure how he knew that, but the knowledge was there, solid and inarguable, and just as certain was the fact that he had lost his chance—perhaps his *only* chance—to go home. Danny turned and started to shuffle slowly down the sidewalk. He would return to the apartment and whatever dope he could score from Birdclaw. It was all he had left to look forward to now.

It was then that he heard the sound—a single note, clear and pure, cutting through the fog. It rang, delicate and high, on the edge of his hearing; he was not entirely sure if it was real or his imagination. But then it came again, a sound like struck crystal, more beautiful than anything he had ever heard before. He turned back and began to wander into the gray mist.

The notes came again, irregularly, as though someone were tapping a fingernail against a silver bell. Danny followed the sound.

It was farther away than he thought, but the sound never faded; it guided him as a chapel bell pulls the faithful to worship. It led him to Chinatown, with its brick buildings and its street signs in English and Mandarin. He passed nervously by huge stone fou dogs that seemed to snarl at him through the fog. And, at last, in a small enclosed garden in one of the many winding back streets,

13

he found his quarry, cradled in the lap of a stone Buddha, swathed in fog.

He bent and looked into the shadowed face, hardly daring to breathe. He saw golden hair framing the features of a girl who could be as young as twelve or as old as twenty. She had been crying, and evidently had just now fallen asleep—a single last tear trembled on the end of her button nose. As Danny watched, it fell to the damp brick below, and the single chime rang out again as it struck.

He stood in front of her for a long moment, unsure what to do next. The fog seemed to coil and move like a living thing. It was absolutely quiet—no sounds of cars or voices. He suddenly remembered Roberto telling him that the area that was now Chinatown had once been a burial ground, and that there were still many unmarked graves beneath the buildings and streets.

Danny shivered in the darkness. He stared at her face; the sight of it seemed, somehow, to lessen his fear. He was reluctant to wake her, afraid that she would once again melt out of his life, this time for good. He did not want to take that chance. At last, however, he bent down and carefully, gently, lifted her in his arms. He was surprised at how light she was—almost as though he carried a bundle of empty clothes. She stirred slightly and whimpered, then settled into sleep once more. Danny turned and carried her out of the garden and into the night.

2

Scott Russell was awakened by the morning sun shining through a crack in one of the venetian blinds. He felt a momentary sense of panic when he realized how late it was, before memory replaced the concern with depression. There was no need to hurry—not today, nor at any time in the future, since yesterday had been his last day at the agency.

Scott lay sprawled across the uncomfortable crease in the couch bed, his eyes closed against the sliver of sunlight. He thought about being unemployed. The concept didn't get any better with contemplation, so after a few minutes he sighed and opened his eyes. The earth had moved just enough in its eternal remorseless spin to shift the orange glare from his face. He glanced at the clock that rested precariously on the arm of the couch. Nine-fifteen; he had slept right through the alarm at eight. Not surprising, considering how drunk he had gotten last night.

Scott heard the distant flat sputter of a motorboat farther out in the water; a few moments later the couch rocked gently in response to the incoming swells. It was a soothing motion; he was half tempted to let it lull him back to sleep. After all, there was no place he had to be. He could stay in bed until his landlord—if that was the proper term for the owner of a houseboat—had him evicted for not paying his rent.

Unfortunately, the rocking motion was making him increasingly aware of his full bladder. He sat up, pursing his lips at the unpleasant taste in his mouth. That and the urge to urinate were the only legacies of the massive bender he had gone on after being fired; Scott was one of those fortunate few who never got hangovers. The dark cloud to that particular silver lining was that he always remembered everything about his rare drinking bouts with painful clarity. This one was no exception. He rubbed a tender spot on his ribs where the barmaid had hit him; not a slap, he recalled, but a painful short jab that had taken the wind out of him in more ways than one. He winced, more at the memory than at the soreness.

He got out of bed and made his way stiffly across the small room. The complicated maze of plumbing that linked the boats to the sewer system had backed up again, and he didn't want to face the chemical toilet he had purchased as a stopgap measure; he hadn't emptied it in the nearby public restroom last night. He was tempted just to pour it over the side, but he had enough troubles without being caught polluting the bay.

He confined his pollution activities to a smaller scale; there was a crack between two warped floorboards near the door that revealed the water beneath. After he was through, Scott pulled a pair of pants from the tangle of clothes, newspapers and empty take-out food containers that littered the floor. Half-dressed, he went outside.

It was a clear morning in Sausalito, though he could

16

see a fog bank like a solid gray cliff over part of San Francisco. Behind him the picturesque little town rose in wooded coziness up the hills. All about him were the arks, as they were known, some floating in placid water, others marooned temporarily in the green muck of low tide. A more bizarre collection of craft could not be imagined; from where Scott stood he could see houseboats ranging from little more than shacks mounted on pontoons to strange, decadent floating palaces festooned with stained-glass windows and Byzantine minarets. He stood on the deck for only a minute or two, his breath forming clouds in the chill air, before making his way to the pier and the kiosk that held the rows of mailboxes.

There was nothing in his box save a few circulars addressed to "Occupant" and an overdue phone bill. Scott went back to his boat, shivering. It was one of the less imposing ones: a two-room shanty constructed mostly of wood and corrugated tin siding. He dropped the mail in one of the piles on the floor and wandered into the kitchenette, where he put a kettle of water on the hot plate. He picked up a shoe lying near a dirty plate and swatted half-heartedly at a couple of water bugs in the sink. Then he put the shoe on and began a search for its mate.

By the time he found it the kettle was whistling. He lifted it from the hotplate, but instead of making a cup of instant coffee he looked out at the room. It looked unfamiliar in the early morning light. On a shelf by the door sat a lava lamp he had bought a couple of years ago out of nostalgia for the one he had had in college. He never plugged it in anymore—the inside had somehow become coated with some vile green substance. Over the couch bed was a yarn-and-pin mandala made for him by a woman with whom he had lived for three months in 1972.

17

It was the only thing he still owned from that long ago. Staring at it, Scott could see her face clearly in his mind's eye, but could not, for a long instant, remember her name. Candy, that was it.

The few other pieces of furniture in the houseboat he had bought at garage sales or discount stores. He remembered feeling proud, two years ago, at being able to furnish the entire place for less than five hundred dollars. It didn't seem anything to be proud of now.

"Jesus, what a mess," he said. After a moment he added, "I'm talking about your *life*, Russell; not this place. This place is a *sty*."

Though he had lived alone for most of his adult life, he was not in the habit of talking to himself. The words seemed to hang in the silence. What happens now? he wondered. His job at the Golden Gate Detective Agency had been nothing spectacular; the pay had been slightly more than minimum wage, plus mileage and equipment. Not much to brag about for a man nearing forty. He had been fired for a very simple reason: he had not been very good at his job. He had gotten the position largely on the recommendation of a friend who was also a friend of the owner. Scott hadn't even particularly enjoyed the work, and he certainly had had no romantic illusions about being an operative; he had never even read a detective novel until after starting the job.

The job had not been glamorous. It had consisted mostly of surveillance, which translated as long hours spent sitting in parked cars watching houses and apartments and then filling out reports about it. He had never carried a gun and had never wanted to. Still, it had been fun on infrequent occasions. It had even been a way to impress women once in a great while. But, most importantly, it had been a way to pay rent and buy groceries.

18

And now he was unemployed, with two weeks' severance pay and two hundred and thirteen dollars in the bank. What, Scott wondered, would Philip Marlowe do now?

He didn't know, and didn't particularly care.

The phone rang.

It seemed so out of place, there in the quiet morning light, that he let it ring again before he thought to pick it up. *Let it be my boss saying he's reconsidered. Let it be Bay or some other agency with an offer* . . . "Hello?"

"Russell?" The voice was unfamiliar. There was a faint long-distance hum on the line.

"Speaking."

"Edward Thayer."

Scott blinked in surprise. "Ed! This is quite a surprise." That was putting it mildly; he had not spoken to Ed Thayer since the two of them had attended college together back east nearly twenty years ago. Thayer had been a Vietnam vet in his mid-twenties, finishing his education with the help of a VA loan. Hearing the man's voice now, with the sun coming through the window at a strange angle and his life at such loose ends, had a distinctly surreal quality to it.

"Reilly tells me you're a private detective." Thayer's impatience with conversation and social niceties evidently had not changed over the past two decades. Scott remembered Reilly as another of their college friends with whom he had kept in touch by phone occasionally.

"Well, uh, not exactly . . . I work for an agency. I mean, I used to—"

"Doesn't matter. I've got a job for you." Thayer sounded annoyed, and also worried. "I want you to find my son. His name is Danny and he's been missing for six months now. He's somewhere in San Francisco."

Scott had felt a moment of hope when Thayer spoke

19

of a job. Some kind of domestic or camera work, possibly, or maybe roping someone on an insurance dodge. That he could handle. But a runaway—forget it. He knew his chances of finding a kid on the streets were less than zero. "Have you tried—"

"The police?" Thayer sounded disgusted. "Of course. And I'm sure you can imagine just how helpful and effective they've been."

Scott tried to think of a way to end the conversation gracefully. "A missing person case—particularly a runaway—is a damned hard job, Ed. Anyway, I'm afraid I'm no longer with—"

"I'll make it worth your while. What're your rates?"

The surreal feeling was growing stronger. Scott realized with a flash of wry amusement that he had no idea what a private detective would charge. "Actually, I don't—"

"I'll give you a hundred dollars a day plus expenses. Is that fair?"

Scott felt suddenly dizzy. He tightened his grip on the phone carefully, as if to ensure that nothing happened to the connection. "Uh, well, Ed, I think—"

"I won't waste time on nickel-and-dime bargaining, Russell. Name a price and I'll pay it. I want my son back."

Scott swallowed, wondering how far he dared go. "A hundred fifty a day," he said, relieved to hear that his voice sounded firm. "Plus expenses."

"Fine. What do you need to know?"

Scott moistened his suddenly dry lips. What he needed was a moment to marshal his thoughts. "I'm in the middle of a meeting right now, Ed. Can I get back to you?"

Thayer gave him a Los Angeles number. "When will I hear from you?"

"By noon, I promise. And thanks for—"

"I'll cancel a few appointments. I'll be here." There was a click, and it wasn't until he heard the dial tone that he realized Thayer had hung up.

He hung up also, carefully, handling the phone like a fragile, delicate thing. He stood for a long moment, his mind held deliberately blank, before he put the kettle back on the hotplate.

A hundred and fifty dollars a day, he thought wonderingly. Two days at that rate would pay his rent. A week's worth, plus his severance pay and savings, could keep him going for more than three months. It was a godsend. He was no longer depressed—in fact, he felt sufficient optimism and enthusiasm to start cleaning the houseboat.

"I'll be a son of a bitch," he said softly. "Just call me Sam Spade."

AS HE GATHERED HIS laundry off the floor, Scott reviewed his options. He had few marketable skills; in fact, sometimes he felt it was a wonder that he had managed to survive this long. He had changed his major several times in college, from music to English to business. Once out of college, he had worked at a variety of small-time positions—among other things, he had been the assistant manager of a theater for three years until the chain that owned it went bankrupt; and then he had worked as a proofreader for a publisher of technical books. When that job went south, he became a shipping and receiving clerk in a bookstore. A few other desultory positions came after that; he honestly could not remember them all at the moment. At one point he had been reduced to driving a cab. At last had come the job at the detective agency. Between jobs he had spent long periods on unemployment. Things had never gotten so bad that he had been unable to keep a roof over his head or food on the table, though it had been pretty tight at times.

Obviously, his life was long overdue for a change. Drifting from job to job had been all right for a time, but now that he was pushing forty it was starting to get very old. Though he possessed a BA in English, it had been earned more to keep him out of the draft than as a means to gainful employment. He had never been able to dedicate himself to a planned career.

He hadn't always been so overwhelmed by life. He remembered being in college, the heady sense of riding the youthful wave that was going to change the world and usher in the Age of Aquarius. He had wanted to be a teacher then—but not like the narrow-minded establishment-owned drones who passed for professors; he regarded them with contempt. Teaching was a holy chore, a chance to help sculpt new minds, to build the future—he wanted to instill people with the desire to learn, with the joy of discovery. Later on he had changed his plans, decided to be a social worker. He had even gone so far as to write to the Peace Corps, but had never followed up on it.

That was his problem, had always been his problem. He had never followed up on anything. Instead of riding the demographic wave, he had let it carry him where it would, and finally he had been cast ashore here, at the midpoint of his life. *In an oil slick,* he thought wryly, pushing the metaphor to its ridiculous limit.

Perhaps now, however, it would finally change. Perhaps with the promise of enough money coming in to pay his expenses for a few months, he could finally break out of this endless cycle.

Certainly Ed Thayer didn't seem to be having the same problems with his life. From his remark about canceling appointments and his money-is-no-object attitude concerning Scott's fee, it seemed fairly obvious that Thayer had become quite successful. Of course, Scott thought, no life is without trouble, and no doubt Thayer would trade all of his worldly gains to get his son back.

Scott stopped in the middle of his cleaning, struck by a thought. In his excitement about the prospect of money he had not given much consideration to his end of the bargain. He had assumed that he would simply take this manna from heaven and use it to support himself while he tried to find employment. There was very little chance of finding Thayer's son, after all—the man had been watching too much television if he thought otherwise. Dropping a child with no paper to speak of attached to him into a city the size of San Francisco was like setting a mouse free in Muir Woods and then expecting to find it again.

Of course what he intended was dishonest. But, he told himself, these were desperate times. Thayer could afford to spend a few hundred dollars on Scott's welfare. His son would stay lost either way, after all.

Still, it didn't feel right.

Scott went out again onto the boat's tiny deck. The fog was beginning to lift across the bay; he could see the docks of the Embarcadero and, beyond that, the skyscrapers of downtown beginning to emerge from the mist.

He wondered: *Have I no self-respect left at all?*

It wasn't even that he felt he owed anything to Thayer for taking his money—but he did owe something to himself. He had been a lousy operative for the Golden Gate Agency, but it wasn't for lack of trying. He just wasn't cut out to be a detective.

And that was the heart of it: he was almost forty and he still didn't know what he was cut out to be.

Staring across the green mud and the blue water,

Scott decided on a course of action. He would make an effort to find Danny Thayer, knowing full well that it was fruitless. But he would also reserve part of each day for job-hunting. It seemed a realistic compromise between conscience and survival.

That decision made, he suddenly realized that he was hungry. He glanced at his watch. It was ten o'clock; there was time to take a leisurely breakfast at the Sand Dollar Coffee Shop up on Bridgeway before he called Thayer back.

He finished dressing and put on a windbreaker, shaking his head in wonder at the situation. *A pity I don't have a trenchcoat,* he thought with wry amusement as he headed up the pier.

3

Danny awoke abruptly. At first he was confused about where he was; then he remembered. He looked at the mattress on the floor across the room, fully expecting the girl he had brought back to the hotel last night to be gone, and with her his dreams of going to Middle Earth.

But she was still asleep in almost the same position as he last remembered her, cuddled in the huge pea coat. Danny felt a wave of relief that made him momentarily dizzy.

He stood up, stiff from sleeping on the floor but more excited than he could recall being since the day he ran away from home. He thought of going down the hall for the bong in Roberto's room—a hit usually relaxed him—but stopped, realizing that this was no time to get stoned. Besides, he was afraid to take his eyes off her, afraid she might awaken and disappear again.

By the time he had gotten back to his room at the hotel with her, everyone had been asleep—even Birdclaw, who usually didn't crash until dawn. Danny had wanted to wake up some or all of them to tell them of the miracle he had found, but carrying her that long distance had exhausted him. He had intended to keep guard over her, but realized now that he must have fallen asleep almost immediately.

Moving carefully so as not to disturb her, Danny crossed to a bucket full of water, dipped his fingers into it and rubbed his face. The fog outside made the light in the room dim. He debated turning on the light—Roberto had tapped electrical power from the pole outside—but decided not to. In truth, he was somewhat afraid of waking her up.

He had not given much thought to what he had done in bringing her here. It had taken quite a while to carry her to the condemned hotel south of Market, and what little he remembered of the walk had a dreamlike quality to it. All he knew was that he could not let her out of his sight again. He wasn't even sure why, in the cold gray light of day. But he knew, deep within his bones, that she was the most important person ever to come into his life.

The chill water on his face made Danny feel considerably better. He decided that he could chance leaving her alone long enough to see if Roberto was awake. Roberto always listened to his stories about Middle Earth with great interest, and always said that there was no reason why they couldn't be true, because everyone knew that there were other dimensions just like the ones in science fiction movies. Roberto would understand why he had brought her here . . .

Danny turned around—and froze. She was awake, and watching him with eyes as bright and blue as the bay on a summer afternoon.

For a long moment neither of them moved. Danny felt that his brain was on hold—he had no idea what to say or do next. The only thought that ran through his mind was *Please God, don't let her disappear.*

And then she laughed.

Had he begun to wonder if he had imagined the silver shattering sound her tears had made against the pavement last night, her laughter would have convinced him otherwise. Danny had heard a baby laugh not long ago, during a sunny day on the Marina Green in Pacific Heights. The infant had been watching his father guide a red kite against the clear blue sky, and the pure joy and delight that had come from his throat had been more beautiful than anything Danny had ever heard—until now.

He stared at her, aware that his jaw was hanging loosely, feeling slow and stupid and made of mud as she bounced off the mattress in one quicksilver motion, leaving the pea coat on it. He was immediately and hopelessly in love with her. She pushed her long straight hair back from her face, revealing ears with delicate, Spock-like points, and regarded him with a look of delighted amusement.

"Well," she said, and her voice was as pure and melting as her laughter had been, "it looks like there *is* a purpose to things after all."

The only thing he could think of to say was, "There is?"

"Of course," she replied. "Why else would *you* have found me just when I needed help the most?"

"I . . . don't understand," he said slowly. "I saw you last night—and then you disappeared . . ." He hesitated, hoping she would comment on that, but she simply kept watching him and smiling. Danny was momentarily confused; *had* he seen her vanish, or had it simply been the fog and his imagination? He continued uncertainly: "Uh—I sort of concentrated real hard, and then I saw you again."

"Exactly. I was scared at first, I'll admit—I didn't recognize you." She stepped forward and seized his hands in hers; Danny felt a pleasant tingling in his arms. She was close enough for him to smell her, and she certainly did not smell like most street kids he knew. There was the faint scent of some sort of spice, clean and sharp—it might have been perfume, but somehow he doubted it.

If her closeness was intoxicating, however, what she was saying was confusing. She acted like she knew him. The thought raised a great surge of hope in Danny's heart—if she *was* a fairy, did that mean he had been right all along in his belief that he was too? Danny glanced at the wall over the mattress, where hung a tattered poster of an unbelievably pastoral landscape, with the single word "Faerie" and the photographer's name in tiny print along the bottom margin. To go there, to feel the bright green grass under his feet, to leap into the clear air and fly the way he had once felt he could . . .

He started to be afraid—things were moving too fast. "Hey, wait a minute," he said, taking a step back. "I don't know what you're—"

"Hey, dude, what's goin' on?"

They both turned toward the door, where Birdclaw was standing, wearing only a pair of dirty, torn Levi's 501s. His thin, nearly concave chest seemed the color of a mushroom in the dim light, and his hair, which he had neglected to spike with soap this morning, was drooping like a rooster's feathers. He held a joint in his mutilated right hand, which he used to gesture in the girl's general direction.

Danny felt a moment of fear—even as stoned as Birdclaw obviously was, he could not help but realize that this was no ordinary street waif. Though Danny had initially wanted to share his discovery of her with all of them, now he was afraid of what their reaction would be. They might not understand, might be afraid, even hostile . . .

"Listen, Danny just let me crash here last night. You got a problem with that?"

Danny looked from Birdclaw to her again, and stifled a gasp of astonishment. The girl who stood before him now was the same, and yet markedly different. Her hair was dull and stringy, as though it had not been washed in weeks; her skin was sallow and showing the effects of malnutrition; her eyes were dull and suspicious. The elfin tips of her ears were gone; the only thing extraordinary about them was how dirty they were.

When she spoke again, it was the voice he was familiar with, and yet different, with an unpleasant harshness to it. "What happened to your hand, man? Dog bite it off?"

Birdclaw blinked, somewhat taken aback by the hostility. He glanced at Danny. "Jesus," he mumbled as he turned back toward the door, "what dumpster'd you dig *her* outta, Danny? A real winner."

"Piss off, asshole!" she shouted after Birdclaw as he stumbled off down the dark hallway. Then she turned and grinned at Danny—and once more she was the elfin beauty he had seen crying in the fog last night.

"Why'd you do that?" he asked.

The grin grew even more mischievous. "Just because you can see me as I really am is no reason to let anybody else do it."

"Yeah, well, okay—but you didn't have to be so mean to him. I mean, Birdclaw's all right. He gives me dope lotsa times."

The grin faded. "I'm sorry. I don't want to make you mad at me. Not you, of all people."

29

She looked so contrite that Danny felt flustered. "Aw, that's all right . . ."

"It's obvious that the Lady led you to me. I had reached the bottom—I need help, and so do the rest of the scatterlings who were left behind. You know what you can do—why should we waste time talking?" She took his hand and began to pull him toward the door. "Come on—we'll find the others and go home!"

Danny hung back, completely confused by now. "I don't know what you're talking about! I don't even know your— Hey, wait a minute. I don't know your name; how'd you know mine?"

Her only answer to that was another wide smile. Her grins were amazingly infectious; he could not help grinning back. "Sorry. You can call me Robin." She turned back to the bed and picked up her coat. "Please—let's go now. I've been much too long in this city and this world." She gestured to the poster. "I can hear the Hollow Hills calling; can't you?"

"Well, yeah—I mean, I guess so. But wait—" Robin was starting toward the door; Danny reached for her arm, but stopped short of actually touching her. She looked questioningly at him.

Danny took a deep breath. "Look, I don't know what you want from me. I mean, I brought you here because— because I just sort of *knew* you were special. You are, aren't you? I mean—a fairy?"

It was her turn to look puzzled now. "You should know better than to use that word—and you should know that I am not one of the Sidhe. I'm a scatterling."

Danny was beginning to feel panicky—the same suffocating feeling that used to settle over him when he faced his father. "Look—I want to go back to Fairyland with you. I mean, that's why I brought you here—well, not just that, 'cause you looked pretty unhappy, but I knew you were one of them—whatever you want to call them. I don't know how I knew, but I just *knew*—same way I always knew I wanted to go to Middle Earth . . . I always knew it was there, really *there*," he continued, his confusion supplanted by enthusiasm. "I know everybody who lives there—Captain Kirk and Peter Pan, and Robin Hood, and Batman . . ."

Robin was looking very puzzled now. He continued, the words tumbling out in his effort to make her understand.

"There are dragons, right? And dinosaurs, and zombies, and werewolves. Look—" and he turned, hurrying to the closet. From a dark corner beneath a pile of clothes he fished out an army surplus bayonet. "My sword!" He lifted a toy ray gun in the other hand, his finger squeezing the trigger to release a barrage of blinking lights and rasping sounds. "See? I'm ready for anything! But—I don't know what you want from me. Just tell me, and I'll do it if I can, but . . ."

He trailed off, looking at her confused expression and feeling an awful certainty that he had somehow blown it—that there was some secret password or phrase that he should have said and hadn't, and that she would now simply vanish like a soap bubble or a waking dream. The possibility of that seemed so real that he ran toward her, dropping the ray gun and grabbing her arm. "Don't go. *Please*. I don't know what I'm doing wrong, but please don't leave me behind," he said desperately.

Robin said slowly, "I wouldn't—*couldn't* leave you behind. I know who you are, even if you don't. Whether or not you can still open the gallitrap, I don't know—yet. But we'll find out—together."

Danny nodded, vastly relieved. He still did not understand all that she was talking about, but it was apparent that Robin did not intend to go without him, and that was all that really mattered.

A cough from the hallway beyond the door made him remember the others in the hotel. "I gotta check on Roberto," he said, tucking the toy ray gun in a pants pocket. "You want to meet him? He's my partner on the street, 'cept he's been sick."

Robin looked dubious at first, but then the by-now familiar grin spread over her face, and she shrugged as if to say *why not?*

The hallway was drafty, with cold tendrils of fog drifting lazily through a broken skylight. The floor was littered with trash and broken glass, and the ripe smells of marijuana and beer permeated the air. Roberto's room was at the end of the hall. It was furnished, like Danny's, in furniture salvaged from trash bins and the sidewalk. Near one wall was a cheap weight bench, a barbell and a set of plates. The plastic coverings of the latter were cracked, revealing molded concrete beneath.

Roberto lay on his mattress, shivering under the covers. He looked worse than yesterday, Danny noticed with concern. Perhaps it was more serious than food poisoning.

Roberto opened his eyes and looked up as Danny sat in the folding chair by the side of the bed. He took Roberto's hand in his, noting how clammy and weak it felt. "How you doin'?" he asked.

"I feel like shit," Roberto mumbled. "Where the fuck you been, you little asshole? You're s'posed to be takin' care of me."

"I'm sorry, Roberto. I been tryin' to make some money for us . . ."

"Y'got enough to buy some booze? I think I'd feel

better if I had some beer." His gaze shifted to Robin, who had come to stand behind Danny, and his eyes narrowed in suspicion. "Who's she?"

"Just a friend," Danny said, sure that Roberto was seeing the same version of Robin that Birdclaw had seen. He felt somewhat nervous; Roberto's sickness had put him in a bad mood, and Danny was unsure how he would react to Robin. He went on rapidly, "I met her last night. She needed a place to squat."

Before Roberto could respond Robin stepped forward, brushing past Danny, and laid her hand on Roberto's forehead. "Hey, what're you doing?" Roberto demanded.

"You're sick," she replied, as though that were sufficient explanation for her action.

Roberto started to push her hand away, but stopped. Danny looked over Robin's shoulder. He was fascinated by the sight of her hand on Roberto's forehead—why, he wasn't sure. But *something* seemed to be happening. Her hand did not glow or shimmer like magic in the movies and cartoons did. Yet there seemed to be something going on nevertheless. For some reason Danny thought of what it was like to stare into an ultraviolet lamp—the way his eyes seemed unable to see all of the light. This was like that, only he couldn't see any of the light. Still, he somehow knew it was there . . .

Robin lifted her hand. Roberto had closed his eyes—his face, which had been tense with pain and anger, was now more relaxed than Danny had ever seen it. He realized that Roberto was asleep.

"He'll get better now," Robin said. "A good thing I touched him—otherwise he would have soon died."

She was looking at him intently, as though she expected some response. "Well, uh—thanks," was all he could think to say.

33

"You owe me for saving him," Robin said. "Will you do your best to help me now, even though you've forgotten the way? Believe me, it's as much for your benefit as it is mine."

"You mean open this gallitrap thing for you? But I don't know how to—"

"You'll remember," she interrupted. "No matter what it takes, I'll see to that. You're our last hope, Danny. The Fair Realm has drifted away from this one over the centuries, but those of us who live in both didn't expect the portals to close so quickly and so firmly." She sighed. "I had given up all hope of seeing the Tuatha de Danaan again before you found me. We can't survive for too much longer in this world."

Danny was not sure why he hesitated. This was what he had wanted all his short life, ever since he could remember: the opportunity to flee this dreadful world for a finer, purer one, a world of beauty and adventure and perhaps even love. But now that the chance was offered, he was frightened. It was all happening too fast. As much as he longed to abandon the hopeless life he led for a better one, it was familiar and, to a degree, comfortable. What he was being asked to exchange it for was the unknown.

Robin evidently sensed his uncertainty, because she said, "You must have trust, Danny. It's easy for you to believe that I'm who I say I am, but you have to do more than that—you have to believe that you are who I say you are. Can you do that?"

Danny returned her gaze and saw something in her eyes that he had seen very little of in his life so far: trust. And, though he was very afraid of where she might lead him, he found himself nodding.

"Good! Then let's go."

"Go? Go where?"

She had already started from the room—she stopped and looked over her shoulder at him. "Why, to Middle Earth, of course." Then she was gone, and he hurried to follow.

4

Though the routine was as natural to her as breathing by now, polished and smoothed by nearly twenty years of repetition, still Alice was a few minutes late in opening the doors. After all this time, it still bothered her; after all, a business was a business, and should run smoothly. Nine o'clock to nine o'clock, six days a week—those were the hours. She always awoke at six, had her whole life never needed an alarm clock, and three hours was certainly enough time to shower and dress, feed herself and Mao, get downstairs and open the register—"Isn't it, Mao?" she asked, stroking the cat's back.

After all, it wasn't like she had to commute; her apartment was on the second floor, right above the store. But try as she might, Alice was always five or ten minutes late in unlocking the doors. Her regular patrons were quite used to this, and even said it added to the charm of the place. One expected the chain bookstores in malls to open and close precisely on the hour, they said; those were merely book convenience markets, with all the literary charm of a 7-Eleven. But a real bookstore like the Looking Glass, they said, did not have to be punctual.

Alice Kopfman appreciated the sentiment, but she still felt vaguely guilty about never being able to open exactly at nine. Seven years ago, however, she had hit upon a solution that at least partially solved it as far as she was concerned; she carefully noted how many minutes late she was every morning and kept the doors open that much past nine every night.

This morning the Looking Glass bookstore opened at six minutes past, on a morning surprisingly sunny for this time of year in San Francisco. Only one person was waiting; a college student by the look of him, a knapsack of books slung over one shoulder, wearing his hair cut short over his ears and wire-rimmed glasses. He looked vaguely annoyed at the delay, and Alice resisted an impulse to apologize. Instead she asked him if he was looking for anything in particular. He requested a book on Beckett's plays, and she showed him to the drama section. "If you're interested in existential theater," she said, "I might recommend a few other playwrights—"

"I'm not interested in them," he interrupted her. "I just have to read them."

Alice sighed as she rang up the sale and watched the young man go on his way. "No one likes to read anymore, Mao," she complained to the cat. It was true; so much so that in the past few years she had been hard put, at times, to make ends meet. She had had to let go two people who had worked with her for three years because sales had dropped so badly.

Alice looked sadly at the labyrinth of shelves and bookcases before her, some of which were still slightly disorganized as a result of the earthquake in 1989. Even so, she knew their arrangements by heart: Art and Artists down that aisle; Religions, Drama and Poetry over there; Children's Books by the register, where she could keep an eye on them; Literature and Literary Criticism taking up the entire north wall; the section on Computers by the window. Downstairs were the various Sciences, Medicine, Exercise, and the genre books: Science Fiction, Fantasy, Mysteries, Westerns, Romances and so on. It was an eclectic and cluttered arrangement, and she depended on no catalogues or filing systems to remind her of their locations. She had recently bought a small home computer to help her keep up with bookkeeping and ordering, but the books themselves were in her head, and she liked it that way.

Suddenly happy again, Alice looked about with a smile on her face. The Monet and Charles Bragg prints on the wall reflected sunlight off their shrink-wrapped surfaces; a windchime of seashells tinkled in a faint breeze; a rainbow hovered near the Mythology section, cast by a faceted glass ball hanging in the east window. On the wall behind her hung a quotation by Van Gogh, done in needlepoint for her by one of her customers:

> "I think that I still have it in my heart someday
> To paint a bookshop
> With the front yellow and pink in the evening . . .
> Like a light in the midst of darkness."

Alice had always liked for things to look just as they should, and this morning perfectly fit her perception of how a bookstore should appear. She was aware that she was an essential part of the picture: aging and somewhat chubby, with apple cheeks and gray hair. She looked so motherly, in fact, that people sometimes blushed when they paid for copies of books from the Erotica section.

What would they say, she wondered, if they knew she had once corresponded with Henry Miller and Anaïs Nin?

Mao padded across the floor and leaped up into the bay window, picking his way carefully among the standing bestsellers until he found a spot in the sun large enough to accommodate him. He curled up, his sable coat gleaming in the morning sun. Alice took another sip of her coffee as she looked at him. Mao had been her only companion since Clark had died in 1980. The cat had appeared on her doorstep the day after the funeral, and she liked to pretend that he was somehow linked with her husband because of that, some form of avatar or familiar. Certainly Clark had been much like a cat in his quiet and self-assured ways. Alice talked to Mao much the way she had talked to Clark.

"Well, darling, looks like another slow day," she said now, settling back in the comfortable leather chair behind the desk. "We're a dying breed, Mao. Independent book-sellers are going the way of the dodo and the dinosaur." But at the moment, in the early morning sunlight and the quiet, she could not feel pessimistic. She still turned a fair trade, after all. It was quite a varied and colorful crowd that passed through her doors: students, writers and artists, senior citizens—she watched people from all walks of life come and go.

A funny thing about that . . . Alice prided herself on her ability to keep track of the people in her store, even during heavy holiday traffic. But every once in a great while someone—usually a young person—would come in and she would not see them leave. Yet there was only one door save for the fire exit downstairs, and that was wired to an alarm. It was most puzzling. And even more puzzling: on rare occasions she had sworn that people left whom she had not seen come in.

It was disconcerting and somewhat discomfiting. Alice had decided, though she hated to admit it, and it was a sign of encroaching old age. "It comes to all of us, I suppose, Mao."

Oddly enough, it did not seem in any great hurry to come to Mao. The cat had been full-grown when he had moved in, and now, over a decade later, seemed to have changed hardly at all. Perhaps there was something to her theory about avatars . . .

Alice chuckled to herself and took another sip of coffee. It was nice to have a life so innocent of worries that she needed to make up such imaginative concerns. Bookstores were supposed to be areas of mystery and magic, after all. Still, such thoughts belonged downstairs with the books about elves and aliens, she told herself.

She stood and put a tape into the cassette deck. "I've never understood people who read that sort of stuff, have you, Mao?"

Mao merely looked at her for a moment, eyes slitted and sleepy against the sun's light, as Paganini's *Caprice in A Minor* by Itzhak Perlman filled the cool morning air.

THE DAY PASSED UNEVENTFULLY, like so many other days Alice had spent behind the register. Business picked up after lunch, and at one point she had as many as seven or eight people in the store at once; not bad at all for a weekday. Even more gratifying was the fact that five of them bought books—one man spent over three hundred dollars on a leather-bound set of Proust. Even Mao seemed to prick up his ears very slightly at the sound of the cash register for that sale.

At six past nine she wheeled in the displays of used books from outside, closed and locked the doors, closed out the register, turned out the lights and went upstairs.

41

She made a supper of canned soup and a roast beef sandwich and settled down, with Mao purring comfortably on the arm of the overstuffed chair, to read a few chapters of a book about World War II before bedtime.

It was a comfortable life—not glamorous or wealthy or exciting, but it suited Alice. There were worse places to live than above your own store—particularly when that store was a bookshop stocked with more books than you would ever have time to read. Her one regret was that Clark was no longer there to share it with her—but she had come to enjoy her solitude. She could not imagine beginning another relationship this late in her life. "Besides, you'd be terribly jealous, wouldn't you?" she asked Mao, whose response was to purr so loudly that Alice could hear it—it sounded, she fancied, like the distant roar of bombers' propellers over England during the Blitz.

LATE THAT NIGHT ALICE awoke from a troubled sleep. She rolled over and looked across the small bedroom. The light from a streetlamp and the moon shone through the window, silvering the carpet and furniture. She was reminded, for some reason, of that old animated film, what was it called? *Fantasia* . . . where the fairies had gone skating and flitting about the pond, spreading frost everywhere they touched.

She tried to go back to sleep, but could not seem to close her eyes. She was looking at the bureau, admiring how the cold light played on the wood, when a shadow suddenly cut across it. Huge and distorted, it moved fluidly, black as ink. Alice gasped, and looked quickly at the window—then relaxed with a chuckle.

It was only Mao; the cat had leaped onto the radiator in front of the window, and the angle of the street lamp outside had magnified his shadow on the wall. Mao now

42

settled down on the warm metal, tucking his legs beneath him in that compact crouch cats favor. The moonlight caught the luminous green of his eyes as he looked steadily at her.

It was very quiet. She could hear no traffic outside; nothing, in fact, but the ticking of the clock on the night table. She squinted at the large red numbers. A little after four A.M. Just before dawn, the deepest part of the night, when the world is furthest from its protective fire, exposed to whatever lurks in the gulfs between the stars. Alice blinked, half surprised, half amused, at the penny-dreadful line of thought. It was like something out of one of those lurid horror novels that she reluctantly stocked.

She bundled the blankets under her chin, but sleep would not return to her. Instead, she found herself looking once more into Mao's unblinking gaze. It seemed that when she closed her lids she could still see the glowing green almond shapes of his eyes—they filled her vision, growing larger . . .

Alice sat up with a little shudder. Mao regarded her calmly. "All right, then," she said crossly to the cat. "I guess a cup of tea is what's needed." She put on her slippers and housecoat. "Why don't you go chase a mouse or something?" she scolded the cat. As if in response, Mao leaped down from the radiator and padded beside her as she went down the short hall to her kitchen.

Her apartment was small, with only one bedroom, which Alice did not mind—in fact, she rather liked having each room only a few steps from the others. She pulled the light cord, expecting the kitchen to fill with warm, friendly light, but instead there was a blue flash that made the darkness more intense than ever. She realized what had happened—the bulb had burned out. "God *damn* it!" she said crossly. She was not about to attempt climbing onto

43

a kitchen chair to replace it in the dark—she would have to make her tea without light.

The kitchen was the darkest room in the apartment; there was only one small window, and it faced the building next door. Alice turned on the hall light—it helped somewhat—and put a kettle on. She opened a cabinet to get the tea. A skittering sound from the dark shelves caused her to draw her hand back with a little cry. A roach—one of those huge, repulsive water bugs. She steeled herself and reached in, quickly grabbing the tea tin. "This is rapidly becoming a miserable night, Mao," she told the cat.

She felt somewhat better after her first sip of tea. She carried the cup out into the living room and turned on the lamp. She was tempted to turn on the TV as well just to see what strange programs might be showing at this hour, but decided not to. She was rather enjoying the quiet.

Mao leaped silently onto the back of the overstuffed chair she sat in. Alice could feel the vibration of his purring against her head as she leaned back. The room looked much like the bookstore below; shelves crammed with books, and artists' prints on the walls. It had a strange feeling to it, both familiar and at the same time new, as if she had returned to it after a long trip. Alice supposed that that was due to the odd time of night.

She finished her tea, but still did not feel sleepy. Well, the hell with it then; she might as well have breakfast and start her day. It would be dawn before too much longer. Perhaps this morning, for the first time in years, the Looking Glass would open on time.

She felt a sudden urge to see what the store looked like this early in the morning. Feeling as if she were doing something absurdly daring, Alice opened the door and descended the stairs.

44

The rows of bookshelves and display dumps looked terribly mysterious in the first faint light of dawn. Alice wandered among them, stopping now and then to tuck a volume back in place or straighten a picture. She felt very much at home here; the silence was that of millions of words waiting to be read. She turned on the light to the downstairs section, but did not descend. The rest of her was waking up now, and she realized she would have to seek out the little room in the back in a few moments. Still, she lingered for a moment longer, enjoying the silence. I have done well with my life, she thought. I can think of few nicer things to do in one's old age than to own a bookstore.

She and Clark had bought the store in 1975. It had not been a bookshop then; that had been their dream. It had, in fact, been a dry-cleaning establishment, and they had spent a month redecorating, putting down new linoleum and repainting. Clark had built most of the bookshelves himself, and she had stocked them with their first shipments, putting herself in bed for two days afterward with a sore back. It had been nip and tuck for quite some time afterward, what with mortgage payments and business taxes and all. But they had made it. And Clark had at least lived long enough to enjoy several years of it.

They had met in 1946; he had just returned from the war and had cut quite a dashing figure in his uniform. She smiled, remembering him as young and eager to make his mark in the world. They had lived together for two years before getting married; quite a scandalous situation in those days, but she had never been one to pay overmuch attention to others' definitions of morals.

Clark had not exactly become the whirlwind success he had promised her he would; he had eventually taken a job in civil service, working as a production supervisor at

45

an air force base during the Fifties and Sixties. He had always felt himself a failure because of that, though Alice had assured him repeatedly that she would have been proud of him no matter what he had done. She had also worked at a variety of jobs to help make ends meet, which had only added to poor Clark's guilt. He had loved her madly, but had never known quite what to make of her independence.

She had never been able to make him understand that success, in her mind, was not what other people mandated—it was how you felt about yourself. They had been ostracized by other couples for never having desired children, but it had not swayed their decision to remain childless. So what if they had never been rich? They had been soulmates, partners and lovers for more than thirty years, which was far more than most people accomplished.

Thinking of Clark, as always, made her think of Mao. She realized that the cat was not by her feet, as he had been when she had entered the store. She was standing at the top of the stairs that led to the genre section. Through the window behind her she could see the first rays of the sun. There was a trembling quality to the moment that made her think of blown-glass sculptures. It seemed that she could hear windchimes, faint and far away.

It was then that Mao suddenly leaped past her, brushing against her leg and making her jump. Alice watched in amazement as the cat hurtled down the stairs in great, pantherish leaps. She could not recall ever seeing him run like that before. In an instant he was gone, disappearing among the rows of the fantasy section.

Alice felt suddenly dizzy, as though the world had shifted beneath her. She took a deep breath, and it seemed that for just an instant her lungs were filled with the scent

46

of the sweetest flowers she had ever known. But when she inhaled again, all she smelled was the familiar scents of dust and paper and wood. The moment was over—and when Alice turned around, she saw that the new day had begun.

5

Douglas Francis Craig was drunk again. That in itself was not surprising, even considering the time of day, which was not quite nine A.M. If one was an early riser, which Craig had been all of his life, one could down quite a bit of liquor before noon, and this he did quite frequently. His favored drink was Chivas—after all, if one is to be an alcoholic, one should at least have style.

He filled another glass with amber liquid and settled back in his chair before the picture window of his home. The veil of mist that covered the bay was threatening to lift early today; he could see a single sailboat, like a white handkerchief in the pocket of a gray suit. He had never cared overly much for the morning view—from a professional stance, he felt much more could be done with the evening, when the light of the Pacific sunset burnished the water, and thousands of windows in the Berkeley and Oakland hills glittered like broken crystal.

The taste of the scotch was pleasant. He considered himself fortunate; many alcoholics he had met during his periodic remorseful sessions at AA had described how much they hated the taste of their addiction. One woman had told of the lengths she had gone to once to disguise the taste of whiskey, including adding chocolate to it. "It tasted so bad I could hardly finish the second glass," she had said. Craig had not been to one of the meetings in years; not since he had come comfortably to terms with the fact that he was committing suicide a bottle at a time.

Two weeks ago, while strolling among the columns of the Palace of Fine Arts, he had seen a young woman wearing a T-shirt which read: *I don't have a drinking problem. I drink, I get drunk, I fall down—no problem.* Hear, hear, Craig had thought. It seemed a much more sensible refrain to grow accustomed to than "Hi, I'm Doug and I'm an alcoholic."

Still, it was almost embarrassing, in a way—the classic cliché of the failed artist turning to drink. But, as he had told auditoriums full of attentive art students more than once on various lecture junkets, clichés are clichés because they ofttimes contain considerable truth.

Craig tilted the glass and drained its contents. "Everybody should believe in something," he said pleasantly to the view before him. "I believe I'll have another drink." It was another T-shirt aphorism of which he was fond. He stood and crossed the thick Persian carpet to the wet bar.

He regarded himself in the bar's mirror as he poured. Liquor had not been unkind to his appearance. He had escaped the mottled complexion, the skein of burst capillaries that marked so many heavy drinkers. The only visible mark it had left on him was his thick, wavy mane of white hair. A lifetime spent climbing and hiking in pursuit of his art had left him still looking quite fit at sixty-two. No, he thought, as he raised the glass in a toast to his image, he could not complain about what liquor had done to his

50

appearance. It had ruined his marriage, alienated his daughter, cost him many friends—but it had not ruined his looks.

It was tempting to blame the disintegration of his career on it, too. But he knew there was a wholly different reason for that.

He used to play games with himself about drinking, used to try to fool himself. "I won't drink before five." That was a popular one. He had actually stuck to it a few times. It had taken him many years to reach a sort of besotted equilibrium in which he was pleasantly drunk most of the time and still able to keep the morning shakes and nausea from becoming too bad. The cure for all that, of course, was simple and poetic.

He had been, for a time, considered one of the premier landscape photographers in the country. He had been compared often to Ansel Adams; both had shared a reverence for such pioneers of photographic realism as Strand, O'Sullivan and Jackson. He had had ambitions, when he was young—so long ago it seemed now!—of being mentioned in the same breath as these giants and others, of creating classics of photographic art. Nothing had seemed impossible then. And he had gone quite a considerable distance toward achieving that goal. He had traveled around the world several times, photographing such varied locales as the Himalayas, the Mato Grosso, the Gobi, and even the Antarctic. He had been artist-in-residence at the School of Fine Arts in San Francisco for several years. During the Sixties, posters of several of his works had proven immensely popular with the youth culture, and the resulting revenue had left him quite well off.

This was fortunate, because at what many considered the height of his career, Craig stopped photographing.

51

He never explained why. He never told anyone about the circumstances involving the shooting of his last and most famous study, called simply "Faerie."

Craig tasted the scotch again as he thought about it. He remembered it very well—even during the worst of his drunks he could remember it.

It had been near midnight, in the Muir Woods; he had gone out to catch a spectacular half moon framed by the redwoods. As he was preparing the shot, he heard the laughter behind him.

At first he thought it was children, or hippies using the woods for some clandestine rendezvous. But there was music as well—and not the heavy, driving rhythms that constantly filled the air of the city these days. This music was light, airy and unidentifiable—it sounded now like a mandolin, now like a harpsichord, and now like instruments he had never heard before. Craig turned—and glimpsed through the woods a shimmering, wavering circle of light. It spun like a sparkling hoop in the air, shifting its angle constantly.

The camera and the shot forgotten for the moment, he crept forward, peering through the bushes. The hoop now appeared to be made of tiny, individual elements, whirling at uniform speed. Craig stared, mesmerized—it looked like a ring system spinning madly about some invisible miniature planet.

He took another step forward. The elements composing the ring were luminescent, glowing with a pearly radiance. Their movement blurred them, but he could make out the flicker of hundreds of tiny wings. Fireflies, then, or some other form of insect engaged in some strange, unknowable behavior. Odd how their buzzing sounded like laughter and music . . .

What a picture it would make!

52

Craig carefully backed up to his camera. As quietly as he could, praying that the delicate phenomenon would not dissipate, he moved and releveled his equipment, made the necessary adjustments and locked the standards. He peered through the ground glass at the upside-down image. He was preparing to insert the film holder when it happened.

In the center of the swirling ring appeared a dot of luminescence, an intense focus of golden light, bright enough to dazzle his night-adjusted vision. It *expanded,* rushing toward him as the sparks that formed the ring abruptly flew off in all directions. And within that light he could see . . .

Craig gasped. In the reversed ground-glass view was another world—a world more beautiful than anything he had ever seen or photographed or dreamed. He stared, enraptured, at the gentle hills forested with strange trees, at the distant waterfall and the mountains. He inhaled air that made the crisp, wood-scented breezes of Muir seem like the heavy atmosphere of a bar or locker room.

Compositionally speaking, the dry shot before him was perfect—the relationships of all the elements within were exquisitely balanced. He could not have asked for a better angle from which to shoot. Almost without thinking, he inserted the holder, closed the shutter and set the aperture. Then he exposed the film.

As he did so, he found himself suddenly surrounded by the twinkling motes of light that had formed the ring. They fluttered about his head and face, their laughter like tiny silver bells. He felt them tugging at his hair and the collar of his coat, urging him gently forward.

They were not insects. They were tiny people, winged people, their faces sharp and fey and full of mischief. They were naked and sexless, as delicate as Dresden china. One

53

hovered for an instant before his eyes and locked gazes with him. In that instant Craig remembered the first time he had looked into his infant daughter's eyes, when she had been no more than a day old, and how he had been struck by their alien appearance. They were like doll's eyes set in a living face; the muscles controlling them had not yet learned the subtle shifts and movements that convey the myriad shadings of emotion. The mind behind them was a tabula rasa—aware, alive, but unthinking. So it was with the eyes of this creature now before him.

They pulled him forward with a hundred tiny tugs, urging him toward the opening that hovered impossibly in midair, leading from the nighttime world of man to the twilight world of—where? Craig felt an almost overpowering yearning to go, to explore, to see what wonders lay beyond those hills. But he was afraid. He hung back; then, panicking, he waved his arms, batting at the swarm. They avoided his flailing movements easily, and the laughter changed to sounds of disappointment and derision.

Then, as one, they left him, spiraling in through the gateway between the worlds, which shrank after them, irising shut in a moment and leaving him with only the bright afterimage of what he had seen. The music was gone, the laughter was gone, the world he could have visited and explored was gone—gone forever, Craig knew. And he dropped to his knees in the thick rich humus, feeling the tears begin.

They had never really stopped, though now they were composed more of alcohol than of saline. Douglas Francis Craig looked at the enlargement on the north wall of his study. He had named it "Faerie"—he had had no doubt, later, that it was an accurate title. It was the only piece he had ever shot that had required no manipulation of the negative, no adding or subtracting of light or shading to enhance the vision. The eight-by-ten contact print had been perfect. The world he had seen had been perfect. And he had let his opportunity pass.

He had never been able to take another picture. He had tried many times, but no matter what scene he framed, it was drab, lifeless, barren. Compared to what he had seen, what he had shot that night in the Muir Woods, no other visualization was worth pursuing.

He knew what it had been. He had suspected at the time, and later research had confirmed it—he had witnessed a fairy ring, a gallitrap, an opening between this world and the land of Faerie. A chance of a hundred, a thousand lifetimes, to take pictures the like of which the world had never seen—and he had let it pass.

The loss had destroyed his career, his marriage, his life.

Craig let the last amber drops trickle from the glass into his mouth. He stared out the window. The fog was beginning to lift now; he could see Angel Island rising out of it, and closer, the barren rock and concrete walls of Alcatraz. It would have made an impressive picture, once upon a time.

He stepped up to the window and tugged on the miniblind cord. The louvered strips of metal descended, cutting off the view. When the room was quite dark, Craig turned back toward the bar.

SCOTT RUSSELL SAT IN an uncomfortable white wrought-iron chair in front of a Italian bakery on Stockton. He was eating a piece of panettone and feeling vaguely guilty about it. A man about his age, wearing shorts and a tanktop despite the cold, overcast day, jogged down the street past him, a pair of Walkman headphones over his ears. The sight did nothing to assuage Scott's guilt; he was

55

always acutely aware how much out of shape he was. An ectomorph, he had never had to worry in his youth about gaining weight—no matter what he ate, he had remained roughly the same weight he had been in high school. Once he had turned thirty, however, he had gained ten pounds seemingly from nowhere, and they had all collected right on his waistline. He had never been able to force himself to exercise—a few painful mornings wheezing through a mile of jogging had been the extent of that. He tried to make up for it by eating healthily—no red meat, cutting down on saturated fats, buying his groceries (when he could afford to) at a health food market in Sausalito. He did occasionally drink, but he did not smoke—more anachronistic behavior for a detective, he thought wryly. But sometimes, as now, his addiction to sugar could not be denied.

He attacked the rest of the fruit bread again. Actually, he told himself, he was probably in better shape than he had been in some time, considering the amount of walking he had done in the last three days. He had awakened this morning with sore leg muscles. Unfortunately, he had very little to show for all that exercise save the possibility of a slightly healthier heart.

Ed Thayer had pouched by Federal Express—after learning to his annoyance that Scott did not own a fax machine—all the statistical information Scott had requested on Danny: height, weight, a recent photo, identifying marks, if any. He had told him that the boy's interest had been primarily in science fiction and fantasy. "Escapist crap," Thayer had labeled it. Thayer hadn't been able to tell him much—it was obvious that the man did not know his son very well.

It had seemed an impossible task, but Scott had not been daunted by that—he had no expectations whatsoever of finding the boy. Still, he could not simply take the money without making something of an effort to earn it. And so he had gone through the motions, doing what he had been taught to do at the Golden Gate Detective Agency. First he had called the SFPD. He had a friend in Missing Persons who knew Scott had been fired, and who had been vastly amused to hear that he was now attempting private work. There had been no report filed by anyone who might have known Danny in San Francisco. He had checked the morgue for any John Does matching Danny's description. Again, nothing. The Food Stamp people also had zip on him. There was no one else Scott could think of to call; he had not established very many contacts at the DMV and other places who might aid him now. And so, having exhausted the telephone possibilities, he had reluctantly hit the streets.

He had shown the picture of Danny around at several bus stations and cheap all-night theaters. At sixteen, Danny was probably too old to interest the chicken hawks who prowled the city looking for new young stock for their cribs. Still, one never knew. All Scott could hope for now was a lucky break.

A boy too young to get a job without fake I.D. faced limited possibilities on the streets. He could panhandle, steal, deal drugs or be a prostitute—those were about the extent of his choices. Scott showed Danny's picture at some of the gay bookstores and bars around Castro Street. This had made for a nervous afternoon—he knew that some rough trade was conducted down there, and being surrounded by males his age with rippling biceps and washboard stomachs who wore leather vests and pants made Scott all the more aware of his own lack of physical prowess.

He sipped his cappuccino and thought about the case

57

so far. He had learned nothing despite all his efforts—hardly surprising. The closest he had ever come to a missing-persons case had been a skip-trace job on an old Polish immigrant who had bought a refrigerator on time and then moved to Oakland with it. But then he had been pursuing an adult, easy to trace by all the paper attached to him. This case, by contrast, was nearly impossible.

The smart thing to do, he told himself, was to drop it now and spend the rest of the time looking for another job. He could send Thayer what Whitaker, his boss at the agency, referred to contemptuously as a "cat-crossed-the-street" report—padded with minutiae and jargon, all of which added up to no leads. Take the money and run. He was no detective, after all—he wouldn't have been fired if he had had any aptitude for the work.

But the odd thing was that he did not want to drop it. It was his first case as a private operative—gotten, true, through a misunderstanding rather than by any deserved reputation, but his case nonetheless. He found himself reluctant to give up. This surprised him, as he had never enjoyed this line of work before. He was not particularly enjoying it now, but that wasn't the point. He wanted to solve this, to find the boy, to prove that Whitaker was wrong, that he *could* do it. Even though Whitaker would probably never know about it.

Scott sighed and pulled a small notepad from the pocket of his corduroy jacket. Again the thought crossed his mind that he really should be wearing a trenchcoat—the weather was appropriate, cold and foggy. *Maybe I can get Thayer to buy me one—I sure as hell can't afford one.* He flipped the pad's pages over slowly, perusing his scribbled notes.

The boy had been a voracious comic book and fantasy fan, according to his father. That gave Scott an idea. He had seen specialty bookstores devoted to the genre on Telegraph Avenue in Berkeley; might there not also be some in the city? It was worth a try, at least. He eyed the rest of his pastry—then, feeling suddenly virtuous, shoved it aside and stood up. Nearby was a telephone booth with a Yellow Pages directory dangling from a chain within it. Back on the case, Scott thought wryly as he headed toward it. Still, he felt oddly optimistic.

BY FIVE O'CLOCK THAT evening, however, his optimism was long gone. He was tired, his feet ached, and he had developed a profound dislike for science fiction. The reason for this aversion was simple: he had spent the last five hours crisscrossing the city, from North Beach to the Mission District to the Haight and back again, showing Danny's picture to the proprietors and customers of three of the four bookstores specializing in the genre. His ancient VW was in the shop again—another constant drain on his wallet—and so he was dependent on public transportation and his feet.

The three places ranged from a garret atop a laundromat to a respectable-sized store. All were decorated with posters from sci-fi films or lurid comic books—one store had a five-foot model of Godzilla, complete with glowing spinal plates, in the store window. The stores' clientele seemed to Scott to be composed largely of either obnoxious adolescents or aging longhairs who liked to discuss orbital mechanics and the personal lives of science fiction and fantasy authors. Scott had learned much more than he cared to know about the strange sexual proclivities of many local writers of the genre. He had not, however, found anyone who could tell him anything about Danny Thayer.

At the moment he was on the Mason Street cable car,

heading up from Washington toward Greenwich. He sat huddled in his coat against a chill breeze coming off the bay. There was one more store to check—a place called Night Circus, on Greenwich just off Columbus. And, he promised himself, even if Danny Thayer was standing in the window with a goddamn luminescent spine, he was going home to bed after this. He could not recall when he had felt so tired.

It was not the unaccustomed exercise, or even the many false leads—his short time with the agency had taught him that detective work was almost as frustrating as it was boring. What was exhausting was the amount of mental effort he was putting into this. He had been doing his best to think like Danny, to identify with him, in hopes of unearthing new clues or ideas. He had made copious notes detailing possible trails to follow. The effort involved was surprisingly intense, but it nevertheless gave him a sense of satisfaction. If he failed to find Danny Thayer, it would not be because he hadn't tried.

He got off on Greenwich and entered the bookstore. It looked like the others he had seen: stacks of comic books and paperbacks on aisle racks, a clutch of oversize art books with buxom, scantily clad cave women on the covers, and posters on the walls. A bumper sticker on the cash register read "Nuke the Smurfs!" It was a sentiment Scott could find no fault with at the moment.

Seated behind the register was a thin, intense young woman with enormous glasses and a T-shirt advertising a comic book about mutated reptiles with a penchant for the martial arts. Scott noticed that a silver tear had been painted on the left lens of her glasses. "Can I help you?" she asked.

Scott brought the picture out of his coat pocket and showed it to her. "Has this guy been in here recently?" he asked, as he had asked several times before, all over the city. He could already see the puzzled look, the slow shake of the head, hear the same reply he had heard before: "No, sorry, don't recognize him . . ."

Except that she nodded and said, "Oh, yeah, him. He's in here all the time."

"He is?" Scott asked in honest surprise. He was so taken aback by the positive response that for a moment he forgot what to say next. "Do you know where he lives?"

"Not really. He's just one of the comic book fans, you know. Doesn't buy much of anything; I don't think he has a lot of money. Come to think of it, he hasn't been in in a few days. He usually shows up when the new month's stuff comes in."

"Anybody around here know him? Any friends that I could talk to?" Scott could feel the tantalizing lead unraveling in his hands.

"Beats me. He doesn't say much." The young woman frowned. "In fact, I think he's a street kid—he's usually dressed pretty shabbily."

So much for that, Scott thought glumly. "Can you remember anything he said the last time he was in here? Something that might've indicated his plans in the next few days?"

The young woman eyed him with belated suspicion. "Why're you so interested? You his father? You don't look like him."

"I'm a detective," Scott said, fully expecting her to laugh. She didn't, however, for which he was profoundly grateful. "Danny's father hired me to find the boy. Any information you could give me—"

The employee did not appear entirely convinced, but she said, "He's a big fantasy freak. Not too into books—I don't think he can read all that well—but he loves the

61

comics." She pointed to a rack behind Scott, which was stacked with comic books. "Especially this one," and she came out from behind the counter and plunked an issue from the rack.

Scott looked at it. The cover showed a group of medieval characters with pointed ears brandishing swords at an annoyed dragon. He glanced at the back and noticed the name of the publisher and an address in Alameda.

"He talks all the time about going to Middle Earth," the employee said. "Tell the truth, I think his elevator doesn't go all the way to the top. I remember a few weeks ago he came in real excited about a story he saw in the *Midnight Star*—that sleazy tabloid, you know? Anyway, it was all about fairies found in Golden Gate Park, and Danny was all hot to find out if it was true." She shrugged. "That's really all I know about him."

Scott nodded. "Thanks. If you see him again, could you give me a call?" He left his phone number, paid for the comic book and left the store.

Enough for today, he told himself as he headed down the sidewalk. He was getting nowhere fast, but then, he hadn't thought he would. Time to catch the ferry back to Sausalito.

He paused, noticing a newspaper rack on the corner that contained copies of the *Midnight Star*. He dug change out of his pocket and fed it into the coin slot—between this and the comic book he would have reading material for the ferry ride, though of questionable quality.

He glanced at the paper. He had seen it in supermarkets and newsstands before—its news stories were usually concerned with UFOs landing on the White House lawn and diets that promised miraculous weight loss, immunity from cancer and an abundance of sexual energy.

This one was no exception. I HAD BIGFOOT'S LOVE CHILD! proclaimed a headline over a picture of a woman who clutched what appeared to be a bewildered chimpanzee to her bosom. Scott looked for the address of the editorial offices.

They were on Columbus, less than a block away.

Scott glanced at his watch. Five-thirty—they were probably open until six. He hesitated, thinking of relaxing on his couch in his houseboat, drinking a beer and watching TV. Then he sighed and turned left, heading up Columbus.

6

"Oh, *Christ,*" Liz Gallegher said. She rubbed her hand across her eyes and took another gulp of cold coffee before turning the pocket recorder on again. The reedy voice drifted up from the desk to her: "We live primarily in a non-organic society; virtually everything we use today is the product of technology. Except for houses, you see? What are houses made of? Wood! Wood is organic! It's the only major part of our civilization that we construct from organic materials! I mean, we don't build cars from wood, do we? We dress primarily in synthetics now, don't we? But we live in houses constructed from living things! Now, it's my theory that the bioelectric fields of houses exacerbate our animal instincts, filling us with urges to go out and kill others just the way we killed the trees that we used to build the houses . . ."

Liz shut the tape recorder off again and stared at it in despair. Then she shut her eyes and shouted: *"Joe!"*

Joe Frampton poked his head past her office door and looked at her in trepidation. "Yeah, Liz?"

"This interview you did . . ."

Joe grinned in relief. "Oh, yeah, the guy with the tree paranoia. Great stuff, huh?"

"Not to be overly negative about it, Joe, but—it's shit. What the hell am I supposed to do with this?" She waved the tape recorder at him. "You think there's a story in what this loon is saying? 'Wooden houses drive people crazy?' That ain't exactly twenty-four point banner material, Joe. It isn't even back page filler.

"Look." Liz pointed to the dummy for the morning edition. "'Abortion in Outer Space!' *That's* the kind of kickoff story I want. Frank came up with this great piece about some knocked-up teenager getting kidnapped by saucer people who coat-hanger the fetus and eat it. *That* will sell copies!"

Joe looked chagrined. "But this guy—he's *real*. I mean, he lives over in Oakland in this all-plastic house, and he—"

"Joe, reality doesn't enter into this. I don't care if the guy's in the phone book or in your twisted mind, understand? All I want is the kind of story that overweight housewives with pink hair will put down a dollar twenty-five for." Liz tossed the tape recorder at Joe; he caught it awkwardly. "Now *go write me one!*"

Joe exited hastily, all but tugging his forelock. Liz Gallegher leaned back in her office chair, positioning her head so as to avoid the cracked Naugahyde on the headrest. Why had she hired Joe? He wasn't one of the boss's relatives, so she did not even have that excuse—she could blame no one but herself. He was a fairly good copy editor and not too bad on layout, but that was the extent of it. He didn't have the imagination necessary to come up with seriously sleazy stories.

She glanced at the clock on her desk. A quarter to six.

Close enough to dinnertime. She looked wearily at the sections of print and photos spread over her desk, awaiting paste-up. They needed a lead story, and they needed it quickly. Liz sighed. Six years she had been working for the *Midnight Star*. She had started out sizing photos, picking pictures of dead people who were safely beyond legal recourse and matching them to stories about crazed hippie killers, miracle cancer cures, microwaved babies and worse. For the past three years she had been the editor. Hardly the job she would have guessed, back in high school, that she would one day hold. Back then she had had aspirations of being a real reporter for a real newspaper.

She had had one brief taste of it, in college. Though she had graduated from high school in seventy-five, one year after Watergate and the end of the state of mind everyone called "the Sixties," still she had done her share of reporting corruption in local and on-campus politics. She had broken a story about unauthorized hazardous waste disposal by chemistry lab personnel—hardly the sort of stuff to make the national news, but an important story nonetheless.

Liz snorted and stood up, reaching for her purse. It was not a bad job; all it required was a resolute cynicism. She now looked out of her window at a world divided primarily into two camps: those gullible enough to believe trash such as she edited and wrote, and everybody else, who were not much better. The only fun lay in seeing how far she could push them, to what outrageous lengths she could stretch the outposts of reality. She had published a story once about a rapist who, due to a freak mutation, had two penises, and who habitually attacked Siamese twins. Even Deighton, her boss, had a hard time accepting that one, and Deighton's opinion of the public's taste made

Liz look like Pollyanna. The readers had loved it, of course. Liz was now firmly of the opinion that they would believe anything.

She put on her coat and opened the door—then stopped. A man stood there, one hand upraised to knock. He was a tall, somewhat stoop-shouldered fellow in his late thirties, with a tired face. He wore a corduroy jacket, the wale of which was shiny with wear, blue jeans and a shirt. In one hand he had a rolled-up copy of the *Star*.

"Excuse me—are you Liz Gallegher?"

"Yeah. I'm also on my way to dinner, so make whatever this is quick, okay?" She watched him somewhat warily; their readership had been known in the past to visit the offices. Liz always felt that straitjackets and hypodermics filled with Thorazine should be maintained in readiness for such visits.

"My name's Scott Russell. I'm a private detective. They told me downstairs that you were the editor."

"They got that right, at least. What can I do for you, Russell?"

"Probably nothing, Ms. Gallegher. This is a long shot, but long shots are what I'm down to." He paused. "I'm looking for a runaway kid, and I'd like to ask you a few questions."

Liz looked at him. He did not seem dangerous; his eyes didn't gleam and there were no flecks of spittle when he talked. She glanced at her watch. "As I said, I'm going out to eat, Russell. Is this gonna take long?"

"I don't know. Why don't we walk while I tell you why I'm here." He fell in beside her as she headed for the elevator. "I understand you wrote a story a couple of weeks ago about fairies in the park." At her nod, he asked, "What was the basis for the story?"

They were in the elevator now; Liz wondered uncomfortably if maybe she had been a bit too hasty in deciding this fellow was harmless. Still, he didn't look strong enough to injure her seriously before the elevator opened, and both his hands were in view. "I made it up. My grandmother used to tell me a lot of Irish fairy tales when I was a kid; I remembered them. That's all. That's where most of the stories we run come from—right up here." She tapped her temple with a finger.

The elevator door opened and they left the building. For some reason that Liz had never been able to understand, pigeons constantly flocked around the glass doors of the entrance. The sidewalk was limed with birdshit. The birds arose now in a flutter of dirty gray wings as the two walked down the street.

"Let me explain what I'm after." Russell turned up his collar against the wind. "This runaway—he's a kid who believes in fairies. I talked to somebody who said he'd read your story and gotten real excited over it. I know that people who are . . . well, let's say avid followers of papers like yours sometimes contact the staff about things they see in print. I was just wondering if he'd done that to you." He showed Liz a picture of a thin fair-haired boy who, though smiling, still looked forlorn.

"Can't recall him," she said, handing the snapshot back.

Russell nodded as though he had expected the answer. "Okay. One more question—did anything specific prompt you to write that story?"

"Yeah—we needed to fill a twelve-inch hole in the front page. Sorry, but if you're looking for information here, you're shouting down the wrong well. The only yardstick of accuracy we use in these stories is a pica stick."

They were walking up Powell Street now; she stopped suddenly and faced him. A trolley rumbled slowly by, packed with tourists. "Wait a minute, though. My journalistic hackles are rising. This smells like a story, and we need one to put this issue to bed. 'Teenage Runaway Finds Land of Faerie'—it's got heart. I like it. Tell you what: I'll buy you dinner if you tell me all about it."

Russell stood huddled in his coat, looking at her. She could not read the expression on his face. After a moment, he said, "No, thanks," and turned away.

She took a step after him and caught his arm. "Hey, what's your hurry? I mean, I'm sorry I can't help you, but at least you get a free meal out of it. You like sushi?"

He turned back to face her. "Look, Ms. Gallegher—"

"Liz. The only one who calls me Ms. Gallegher is my gynecologist."

"—This case is important to me. I don't want to see it trivialized, particularly not in a paper like this." He was still holding the copy of the *Star*; now he dropped it in a nearby litter basket. "I've got other leads to check out. Good-bye, Ms. Gallegher."

He turned and walked away. Liz watched him go, feeling anger building up inside her. Who the hell did he think he was, anyway? She periodically encountered that sanctimonious attitude toward her work and her paper, and it infuriated her. It was all right for her to denigrate what she did, but she would not stand to hear it from someone else. Especially a pathetic-looking gumshoe.

She followed him, intending to overtake him and tell him off. As she walked, however, her anger began to lose ground to her curiosity. A teenage runaway who believed in fairies? *It's certainly the right town for it,* she thought with a chuckle. There was definitely a story here. She slowed her pace. *Forget Russell,* she told herself. *Go have dinner, and then go back to the office and write it up.*

Or rather *make* it up. The closest she had come lately

70

to real reportage had been two years ago, when she had interviewed the female lead of a film shooting in the city and then extensively quoted her out of context to make it look like she was admitting to lesbianism. Just once, Liz thought, it would be nice to do a story like the reporter she had once wanted to be . . .

Liz realized that she had passed her restaurant. Russell was still ahead of her. She looked at her watch. For some reason, she was not hungry anymore. That was all to the good, actually; she had been trying to lose a few pounds. And it was a nice evening, if a bit brisk. What the hell.

She walked a little faster, just enough to keep him in sight without catching up with him. *A detective, huh? Fine. Two can play at that game* . . .

DANNY THAYER SAT ON a stone bench in the parking lot atop Telegraph Hill, looking up at Coit Tower. He had never seen it this closely before. What he had heard about it was true; it did resemble the nozzle of a fire hose.

Robin sat on the bench beside him. They were waiting; when he had asked for what, she had simply said, "To spread the word." She did not seem quite as happy and carefree as she had back at the Larkspur, but she was by no means morose. She watched the comings and goings of people about them with interest, commenting occasionally on one or another.

Danny still saw her as she really was, and he knew that to others she was just another street urchin. Her ability to cloud minds like the Shadow fascinated him. He wished he could do that—maybe if he didn't look so lost and helpless most of the time, people would not take advantage of him.

He was impatient to begin the journey to Middle

71

Earth, but he had learned over the past few days that Robin could not be hurried. It had, in fact, taken them most of this day to reach North Beach, for she had insisted on stopping countless times to watch people or to window shop. She seemed endlessly fascinated by humanity's doings.

It was getting colder as evening approached—even wearing Robin's pea coat, Danny was shivering. Robin seemed unaffected by the temperature. She was rolling and molding what seemed to be a small ball of light between her palms. Danny stared at it, fascinated. He was about to ask her what it was when Robin suddenly turned and looked beyond the parking lot, where a thick growth of trees covered the hillside. "They're here. Come on!"

Danny hadn't heard anything, but he stood and started after her, picking his way carefully down the loose dirt of the slope past clusters of empty beer bottles and Styrofoam cups, through a hole in the chain-link fence. Ahead of him, Robin disappeared into the darkness; he took a deep breath and followed her.

The evergreen foliage of the trees was thickly interwoven, forming a sheltering canopy. Save for a few glimpses of house lights from the streets below, they were in almost total darkness. Danny could barely make out Robin's form ahead of him as the scatterling slipped between the small boles. The trees were barely higher than his head. More than once he slipped and nearly fell down the steep incline.

Then, suddenly, there was light about him.

It was an eerie, flickering radiance that came from several sources, and all of them, he knew, were scatterlings. Five of them surrounded Robin and him. One fellow, smaller than Danny, was wearing jeans, a tie-dyed shirt, an old cutaway morning coat and a silk top hat. Atop the hat's flat crown danced a tongue of silver foxfire. A girl of elfin appearance wore a miniskirt, boots and a navy coat something like Robin's, but full-length. A necklace of blue stones about her neck glowed. Danny looked at the others. Most had long hair that hid their pointed ears, and all were dressed in similar fashion, with feathered earrings, military jackets, bandannas, vests and patched blue jeans. And all were glowing in some way. A boy dressed all in black, wearing a Velvet Underground T-shirt, had twin flames flickering behind sunglasses. None of the flames gave off any heat.

Danny had to force himself to keep breathing; the excitement threatened to choke him. It was true, had to be true—they *were* fairies! The ball of light that Robin had been playing with earlier might have been some kind of trick, but this could be nothing less than real magic.

Robin faced the one with the top hat. Danny noticed that he had a patch on the fly of his jeans—a coat of arms with a lion on it.

"A round-ears," he said, looking at Danny, his voice mocking. "Are you that desperate for company, Robin?"

"Mind your manners, Patch," she replied. "Open up and let yourself feel him, all of you!"

The scatterlings stared at Danny; he felt naked under their scrutiny. Then he heard a collective intake of breath from them. "A sibhreach," the one in the cloak murmured.

"More than that," Robin said softly. "He's a Keymaster."

The young girl in the feathered earrings, with fire glowing on the tips of her long painted fingernails, stepped toward Danny and smiled. Danny had seen that smile many times, from Shanti and others on the street. Yet, though her body language was provocative, there was something curiously asexual about her, as though she was

73

only going through the motions of being seductive. She gazed long and searchingly at him. "If it's true, he sure hides it well," she said at last. "He looks like nothing more than a raggedy human boy."

"The power is there—all of you can feel it. He's just forgotten how to use it—if he ever knew," Robin replied.

Patch regarded Danny with hostility. He took off his top hat and stuck a finger under the base of the flame, then put the hat back on his head and played with the flame, letting it drip from hand to hand like St. Elmo's fire.

"The gates have all closed," he said, almost as if to himself. "None of us knows a way through. The realms are getting further and further apart."

"We'll die if we don't go back soon," a tall, lanky boy shrouded in a opera cloak said. "We'll die just like humans die." A tiny flame contained within a ring of costume jewelry on his finger jittered nervously.

Patch pointed his finger at Danny suddenly, the cold fire dancing on its tip. "If he has the power, how do we make use of it?"

The boy with the glowing sunglasses spoke then. "Only one thing to do." His voice was almost mournful, in contrast to the playful tones of the others. "He has to believe who he is, and what he is. I say we accept him as one of us and teach him. That's the only way we can all go home."

Danny blinked. Was it his eyes, or were the flames growing weaker? He could barely see the faces of the scatterlings now. Only Robin's face remained illuminated, though not by flames or by any light that he could make out—it was as if she glowed from within. Within a few moments, she was the only thing he could see.

She turned toward him, looking more serious than he had yet seen her. "You heard Puck's suggestion, Danny.

74

Will you join us? We'll teach you the magic of the streets, the scatterling lore, until you remember on your own."

"But I want to go to Middle Earth!" Danny said plaintively. "This isn't fair—if I'd wanted to keep living on the streets I could've stayed with Roberto and Birdclaw and the others!"

"We'll go, I promise. But the way you are now, you wouldn't last five minutes in the Fair Realm—the first time you heard the baying of the Hell Hounds or saw the face of a Gwyllion you'd be begging to return to your world. Let us help you. It's the only way."

"I guess so," Danny said reluctantly. "I mean, I don't have a lot of choice, it looks like."

She nodded, then turned and started back up the hill. Danny scrambled after her, reminding himself that this was what he had always wanted—adventure, excitement, danger. But as he came out of the darkness and into the faint light of streetlamps and stars and saw Robin ahead of him, her small form passing the statue of Christopher Columbus in the center of the parking lot, he did not feel any stirrings of anticipation. What he felt was more like dread.

7

Scott had no idea at first that the woman was following him, and this added to his annoyance with her. He felt insecure enough as a detective without being reminded of his inability to spot a tail. He did not notice her until he had walked several blocks; then he caught a glimpse of her following him reflected in the bay window of a small boutique. He exhaled in anger and exasperation. Not only was he annoyed because she had been a clue that had not panned out—he also did not like her. Her cynical attitude toward her work and toward the world in general grated on him. He had enough problems coping with life; he did not need his suspicions about the futility of it all reinforced, and he could sense that Liz Gallegher would be very good at reinforcing them.

There had been a time when he could have been drawn to her for just those reasons. He would have found her brassiness intriguing; that, coupled with the fact that she was good-looking, with an open, easygoing sort of attractiveness, would have been enough to have embroiled him in yet another disastrous affair. Fortunately, Scott complimented himself, he had progressed beyond that self-destructive stage of his life. He might be lonely now, but at least he no longer let that loneliness lure him into emotional quicksand.

He waited until a crowd of people passed between them and slipped into the recessed doorway that led to one of the second-story Victorian apartments above the shops. When she drew even with him he stepped out and paced alongside her. "You come to this neighborhood for dinner often, Ms. Gallegher?" he asked. The look of surprise and embarrassment that he anticipated seeing on her face would more than make up for the annoyance she was causing.

Unfortunately, she did not look abashed in the least. She simply grinned and said, "I'm a reporter, remember? I don't give up on a story easily."

He stopped and grabbed her wrist. She looked at his hand in mild surprise. "I told you there's no story for you here," he said in what he hoped was a steely tone. "Why don't you run on back to your office and rake some more muck?"

Gallegher expertly twisted her wrist against the weak part of his grip between his thumb and forefinger, breaking his hold easily. "The next step would have been to jam my knee into your crotch, friend," she said, "and you'd be pissing through your nose. Don't pull that macho shit on me, okay?"

Scott rubbed a hand over his eyes wearily. "Terrific, just terrific. Okay, Gallegher, I know what you're going to say. It's a free country; I can't stop you from walking down the street. You're on the trail of a story now, like a hyena after a carcass, and there's nothing I can do about it. Well, fine. But don't talk to me, and don't interfere in my investigation in any way, or I'll—"

"You'll what?" she asked, grinning. He glared at her for a moment before inspiration struck.

"Or I'll make a few calls to a few friends—friends who can give you a lot of shit, Ms. Gallegher. Friends with badges."

She laughed. He felt his face going red. *"You're* going to sic the law on *me?* I'm on a first-name basis with nearly every cop in this town. Some of 'em may not be too happy to see me coming, but they all know who I am and what I do—and frankly, they don't give a truckload of rats' asses. You have to do better than that."

Scott turned away from her, leaving her the clear victor in the encounter. He was standing in front of yet another bookshop, though this one did not appear to specialize in the genres of which Danny was so fond. He pushed open the door and went in, more to get away from Gallegher than for any investigative intent. A string of bells hanging across the inlaid glass jingled as he entered. He wanted to tear them loose and throw them into the street.

The elderly woman behind the counter—actually, she was behind a small wooden desk with a computer perched anachronistically atop it—smiled at him. She looked like a Cabbage Patch doll, Scott thought sourly as he headed past her without smiling back. Little and white-haired and apple-cheeked, wearing a simple print dress. She looked like she should be crocheting a pair of booties for her granddaughter.

The bells jingled again. He looked over his shoulder, then froze. Liz Gallegher was in the store, looking around. Her gaze fell on several posters thumbtacked high on the wall—one of them was a reproduction of the Douglas Craig print "Faerie." Gallegher turned to the desk. "Excuse me," she said to the old woman, "but my friend here"—a casual wave of one hand in Scott's general direction— "and I are trying to locate a young boy. He's fond of books about fairies, and we were just wondering if by any chance you saw him in here recently." She turned toward Scott and smiled. "Scott, show her the picture."

Scott could hear his teeth grinding together even over the classical music playing softly. His legs carried him back to the desk somewhat stiffly, and he had to make an effort to smile as he reached for the photo of Danny Thayer. *It's a good thing I don't carry a gun,* he thought.

The little old lady studied the picture carefully, then handed it back. "No, I'm sorry—I really don't recall the face." Her voice sounded just like Scott thought it would.

"Thanks anyway," he said, pulling his lips back over his teeth in a close approximation of a smile. He took Gallegher's arm somewhat carefully, remembering her last reaction to physical contact. "Let's go, Liz."

"Don't be in such a hurry." Gallegher pulled free of his grasp and looked at the old woman again. "Maybe you could tell us what sort of books kids who are fans of this type of stuff might read."

Scott couldn't tell where her questions were leading, but he was desperate enough that he waited for the old woman's answer.

"Oh," she said, "there are simply tons of fantasy novels and trilogies being published nowadays; it's a real boom time for aficionados of the genre. I really couldn't recommend one over another; they all look the same to me."

Gallegher persisted. "Are there any about fairies in particular that come to mind?"

"Well, there's one that people of late have seemed very partial to. It's called *The City Under the Hill,* by

Donald Everett McTosh. I don't know that much about it. The author seems to be something of a mystery man, according to the press release—no one knows who he is or where he comes from. Sort of the fantasy equivalent to Thomas Pynchon, I suppose." She smiled.

"Do you have a copy of it?"

"Of course. In the fantasy section—that's downstairs. I'd get it for you, but I'm the only one here and—"

"No problem, we'll find it." Gallegher looked at Scott. "Any lead is better than no lead. Come on, Sherlock."

She headed for the stairs. Scott hesitated a moment, then followed. He had to admit reluctantly that her line of questioning had been quite good. But why shouldn't it have been? She was a reporter, after all. It certainly did not mean that she would be any less of a hindrance in this case. He followed her down the stairs, still trying to decide how to rid himself of her.

She had reached the first aisles of the science fiction and fantasy section when he caught up with her. "Listen, Gallegher, just because you think you found something, don't get cocky. I don't want you—"

"Will you knock it off?" she interrupted. "Like it or not, I'm into this now—for the time being, at least. It's better than going back to my office and trying to salvage some other hack's thirty inches of drivel about trash compactors of the gods or something."

"Don't think you're going to horn in on my fee for this—"

"Oh, give me a large break." She looked at her watch. "It's almost six. Just put up with me for this evening, okay? If I can't turn up anything worth pursuing, than it's all yours again. Look, Russell," she continued before he could reply, "just *once* I'd like to crack a real story. I don't care if it's as sleazy as an all-night splatter-movie marathon—

81

just so long as it's got some basis in reality. I'm not after part of your fee; the *Star* pays me enough. I won't get in your way, and I might be some help. Now let's find that book." And she started down the aisle.

Scott hesitated, then shrugged and followed her. What the hell—maybe he had been a bit unbending. After all, there was certainly no law that said he had to solve this on his own—particularly if she wasn't going to horn in on the money. In fact, he admitted reluctantly, he could probably use all the help he could get.

She was holding a copy of the paperback when he caught up to her. The cover was very similar to the other books of this type Scott had seen over the past few hours; a stylized landscape with a hero in medieval garb on it and a dragon lurking in the background. There seemed to be nothing special about it. Gallegher handed it to him and took another one for herself. "If I find anything that might be a clue, I'll call you," she said. She took a pen from her purse. "What's your number?"

Scott hesitated—then, not quite sure why he was doing it, gave her his phone number. She scribbled it in the flyleaf of the book, then took a business card from her purse and handed it to him. "In case you feel like returning the favor. Now, since you won't let me buy you dinner, at least let me buy you the book."

She started for the stairs again. Scott watched her walking away from him and realized he was noticing the way the material of her skirt shifted against her thighs as she started up the stairs. "Oh, God," he muttered helplessly to himself, and followed.

THE STORE WAS QUIET after the young couple left. Alice listened to the music—Stravinsky's *Petrushka*—without really hearing it. She was growing worried about Mao; she

82

had not seen the cat since he disappeared somewhere in the basement. The last glimpse she had had of him was when he had run ahead of her down the stairs before dawn. She must have left a window open—that might also account for that breath of strangely scented air she had noticed, or imagined she had noticed.

At any rate, Mao was gone, and although Alice knew that it was the nature of most cats to take a leave of absence occasionally (and Mao was certainly no exception to that rule), still she was growing increasingly worried. He had never been gone this long before. She was considering asking some of the neighbors if they had seen him, perhaps even posting a sign in the front window. The cat was the only family she had left, after all . . .

Alice sighed and returned to contemplating the shipment she had just received. She had ordered twenty-five copies of *Taoist Proverbs to Live By*; she had been sent instead twenty-five copies of the latest popular superhero graphic novel. After a moment's thought, she reluctantly decided to keep them. They would sell. Unfortunately . . .

DOUGLAS CRAIG WAS BY nature a solitary drinker, but even the most solitary of sorts will occasionally crave companionship, or at least the sight of other people. When this mood settled on him, familiar locales were not enough—Craig wanted new places as well as new faces while he drank.

Over the years he had sampled a great many of the bars the city had to offer, from the elegant lounges of Pacific Heights to the murky watering holes of Chinatown. He rarely returned to one more than a few times. There was a sense of danger and excitement that he enjoyed in venturing into some new and unknown den. He was sensible about it, of course—he avoided places that were obviously dangerous, where a gentleman of his years would be a good candidate for a mugging. In all his explorations he had never had any trouble. He attributed this in large part to the fact that he was a benevolent but not friendly drunk, and also that he knew when to leave the field—he never got so drunk that he could not call a taxi on his own. Craig was proud of this—it was, he felt, a sign of self-control.

On this particular night he was in a small tavern on Cole Street in the Haight-Ashbury district, sitting at the bar and listening to a gay couple at a table nearby discussing the problems of their relationship. It was always a source of faint surprise to Craig—though upon reflection he could certainly see no reason why it should be—that homosexual pairings should have the same complaints and resentments as did heterosexuals. He had always expected their problems to be more exotic and esoteric. Outside of an abiding and wholly understandable concern on the part of one that the other's loose sleeping habits might infect them both with AIDS, this did not seem to be the case.

Craig finished his drink and stood. It was pleasant outside, surprisingly warm for this time of year, and he had decided to walk the few blocks over to Haight and see if there were any other neon signs that might beckon to him—it was only eleven o'clock, far too early to call it a night. Craig left a twenty next to the glass and walked out.

As always, the crisp night air sharpened his senses, leaving him feeling nicely intoxicated but not out of touch. This was particularly pleasant in that it made room for a few more drinks.

He was still thinking about relationships as he walked—specifically, about his marriage, which had broken up nearly fifteen years ago. It had been long enough now that the thought of Bernice, or of his daughter, Terri, filled him with only a vague, almost pleasant, sadness. He still heard occasionally from Terri—she had called two weeks ago from Georgetown to see how he was. He had not heard from Bernice for over a decade. The sharp sorrow that that once caused had faded gradually to a nostalgic regret.

Terri had finally given up trying to convince him to stop drinking—for a congressman's wife, it had taken her quite awhile to learn that some battles are not worth fighting. Not that he blamed her for trying. That was what Bernice had never understood: he had never blamed her for being unable to deal with his addiction, with the systematic destruction of his professional and personal life, as well as their marriage. Indeed, he wondered why she had stuck it out for as long as she had—not that he had wanted her to go. But she was entirely too good and valuable a woman to spend the rest of her life hiding bottles from him.

Still, it would have been nice if it had been otherwise. He had never been mean to her or to Terri—he had simply been irresponsible. There was a great comfort in being able to admit one's inability to be an adult, Craig told himself. In its own paradoxical way, it was a very mature insight.

He found his ruminations had caused him to walk farther than he had intended. He was on Haight now, near a nightclub—he could hear loud rock music blasting from behind the closed doors. With a grimace of distaste, he crossed the street. Though he did not disapprove of that sort of music in principle, he had never been able—with very few exceptions—to stand hearing it for more than a few minutes.

He was suddenly aware of the crowds around him,

composed mostly of young people. Teenagers careened by him on skateboards, or walked in large groups that took up the entire sidewalk, their ill-fitting clothes festooned with heavy jingling chains. Mixed with them were those with longer hair, both young and old, a strange commingling of the past three decades. Laughter, conversation and epithets filled the air. Craig stopped on a corner, watching a jostling, noisy line waiting to be let into a movie. He felt a sudden surprising surge of misanthropy—unusual, for he did not dislike humanity in principle, not even its more youthful representatives. But his memories had engendered in him a desire for solitude. He decided to catch a cab; he would finish his drinking in the privacy of his home.

A group making their way toward him caught his attention from the rest of the crowd—they were all wearing flamboyant clothes from those days when the Haight was a haven for the Flower Children. Though enough of that style of dress could still be seen here, there was something about these young ones that made him pause for a moment—even after all these years of disuse, his photographer's eye was intrigued. They were wearing tie-dyed jeans and shirts, odds and ends of formal clothing, beads, medallions, feathers—Craig found it inexplicably charming. There was an innocence to their faces that shone through, even though they were obviously attempting to look very tough, swaggering along with their shoulders thrown back. Those faces stirred something in Craig—some cloudy memory or feeling that was even more poignant for being unrecognizable.

They turned up a side street, heading away from the noise and crowds, toward the Heights. Craig followed them. He was just drunk enough not to question his reasons for doing so, and he was also just drunk enough not to worry overly about any possible danger. It was as if his feet took over while his mind remained occupied with trying to identify the memory that tugged at him.

The hill they climbed was not particularly steep; nevertheless he could feel his heart beating faster as they approached the end of the block. The crowded Victorians on either side were dark, for the most part—from a window he could hear more rock music playing faintly. *There's no escaping it,* he thought wryly.

He did not know if the youths ahead were aware of him or not when they suddenly stopped on the next corner. Craig hesitated, then realized that he would have to continue on and make his way past them or it would be obvious that he had been following them. He felt suddenly nervous—they looked innocent enough, but that meant nothing. The fear old age has of youth suddenly possessed him, and it was all he could do to keep walking as though intent on a particular destination.

He was only a few steps from them now; they had grown quiet, watching him approach. Craig was not sure now whether it was the steepness of the hill or the fear that made his heart thud in his chest, but the intensity of its beating made him wonder if he was about to drop dead of a heart attack before any of them had a chance to lay a hand on him. Something was going to happen—he could feel it building in the air like a single rising note of music.

Then he was upon them. He was about to turn and go around them when they stepped to either side, opening a path for him. Craig felt a sudden calm replace his nervousness. The die was cast now.

He passed through their ranks and felt them watching him. He kept his eyes straight ahead, determined not to show fear. He could see them in his peripheral vision, however. They were smiling, but not in anticipation or cynicism. There was something very knowing and understanding about those smiles—as if they knew the half-remembered emotion that had urged him after them—knew, and sympathized.

He could not help himself—he turned his head as he passed one of the boys and looked into his face. He was wearing beads, a black T-shirt with the name of a rock band emblazoned on it, and a dark blue military jacket. Though it was night, mirrored sunglasses covered his eyes. Craig could see the distorted reflection of himself and the others in them.

As he looked, the image reflected in the glasses changed.

At first Craig thought it was a trick of the light, or his own imagination. Despite his desire to pass through this gauntlet, he slowed, staring in astonishment. The twin images of himself wavered and flowed like oil on water, reshaping themselves into miniature views of a landscape that was strangely familiar . . .

Craig gasped. It was a vision of the photograph he had taken that night in Muir Woods, two decades ago—the glimpse of Faerie! He came to a complete stop, staring in shock and disbelief at the vivid sight, reproduced somehow on the lenses the lad wore. The latter's smile grew wider—it was mocking and self-satisfied, but somehow gentle as well.

"You could use some magic in your life, old man," he said.

And then, quite abruptly, they were all dancing about him, laughing and whirling, some turning cartwheels, others doing backflips, all with the grace and precision of trained gymnasts—and then, just as suddenly, they were gone, scattering down the street like leaves blown in an autumn wind. Leaving him alone, as the sprites had done so many years ago.

Douglas Francis Craig stood on the deserted street corner, gasping for breath. Gradually the sounds of the city began to seep back into his hearing—the laughter and noise of the cars from the busy street behind him, the music playing behind closed windows. But all of these seemed far away and inconsequential, like the murmur of a television unattended in another room. Running through his mind like a closed loop of film was the sight of the boy's sunglasses changing, becoming the picture he had stared at over a glass in his home every day for so many years. And accompanying it, like a crazed soundtrack, were the words: *It's happened again. And this time I won't be afraid.*

8

Scott read the comic book and Gallegher's article in the *Midnight Star,* which he had picked up at a newsstand, during the ferry ride back to Sausalito. The former had something to do with a dying race of fairies in a crystalline city that was either far in the past, far in the future or in another dimension. It was poorly drawn and written, but there was an innocence to both the story and the art that he found surprisingly touching.

Gallegher's article was neither more nor less than what he had expected: a sensational treatment of a report by a street person of seeing the Little People cavorting in the park. It was better written than he had anticipated, but not surprisingly so, and it offered him no particular insight into the whereabouts of Danny Thayer.

He felt quite depressed after reading them, and stood near the railing staring at the lights of the Marin County town across the expanse of dark water. Who was he kidding? He had no chance of finding the missing boy. He had known that when he had agreed to take Ed Thayer's money; odd that the sense of defeat should seem so crushing now. Tomorrow, he promised himself, he would start job-hunting in addition to this fruitless quest. No one could deny that he had given this case his best shot. It wasn't his fault if his best just wasn't good enough.

THOUGH IT WAS LATE when he arrived back in his houseboat, Scott was not sleepy, even though earlier that day he had felt exhausted. He opened a beer and sat down with *The City Under the Hill* by Donald Everett McTosh, hoping that reading a few pages would remedy his insomnia.

He had never read a fantasy novel before, unless one counted trying several times without success to plow his way through Tolkien's celebrated books back in the Sixties. He was, he acknowledged with a surprising pang of guilt, not really much of a reader at all. The last work of fiction he had read had been nearly six months ago; it had been a detective novel read out of an obscure sense of duty arising from his job. He usually watched TV instead of reading.

Scott opened the book to the first page.

In Tir Nan Og, the City Under the Hill, in the land beyond the Bright Plain, Oberon, a high noble of the Seelie Court, sought audience with Queen Maeve.

Oberon was, like most of his kind, tall and fair, with blond locks and green eyes. He had dressed in his finest for this audience, and even in the dim light that suffused the underground corridors and chambers his robes and capelet sparkled with polished opals, jade, and ivory. Now he stood before the amber throne, head bowed, waiting for the Queen to accept a stalk of brisgein from a hovering ellyllon. Its task completed, the tiny sprite flitted away into one of the tapestried hallways beyond the columns that lined the chamber. Maeve took her time consuming the delicacy before turning her milky gaze, blue and cold as clouded sapphires, on Oberon.

Scott put the book down and took a swig of beer. He had no idea what an "ellyllon" was, and felt absurdly resentful that there might be words and phrases in this with which he was unfamiliar. Still, he was determined to read the first chapter at least. He had screwed up just about everything else he'd set out to do today—he would, by God, accomplish *something* before he turned out the light.

"You asked for this meeting, Oberon. I have granted it against my better judgment."

Now was the time for diplomacy, Oberon thought, and for the most subtle dissembling of his long life. "My queen," he said, "I am aware that my family line has long been at odds with yours. But I swear to you by Eochaid's bones that I have no designs on your throne—in fact, my presence here is in your interests as much as mine, and all of Faerie's as well.

"I have come to ask you to close the gallitraps."

What the hell is a gallitrap? Scott wondered. He thought about getting out the old paperback dictionary he had bought nearly ten years ago, but a glance around the

93

untidy room convinced him that a search for it would be fruitless. He sighed and continued reading.

Maeve's alabaster brows arched slightly, but in no other way did the Sidhe monarch evidence surprise. "And what else may I grant you?" she asked after a moment. "Perhaps you would like me to take dinner with the Duergar, or summon the Fomorians from the mists for a friendly game of chess?"

"Sarcasm ill-becomes you, my queen. I am serious. Look about you." Oberon swept one arm in a wide gesture, including the silent immensity of the dim chamber and the green and quiet hills above them. "Faerie is dying. Long have we tried to hide from ourselves this fact, but we can deny it no longer. Wights who once concealed them-selves in barrows now stalk openly through the land. No longer do we ride on glorious hunts and battles; rather we huddle in our brughs, allowing our weapons to grow rusted and pitted while we dream of past glories. No birds sing; no dances are danced. Time is no longer ours to command; the mortals and we pace side by side toward extinction."

Maeve sat quietly upon her throne, so still as to seem almost a part of it. Only her hair, emerald-green and long enough to flow over the carved amber and onto the floor, stirred and rippled, though there was no wind in the throne room. She said, "And to what do you attribute these ills?"

"To our continued contact with the world of men," Oberon replied promptly. "Over the years

94

they have turned away from the ways of nature. Their path has diverged increasingly from ours. They no longer listen to the sounds of the pipes, or peer through self-bored stones. They are destroying the Earth, slowly but surely. Long ago we began to withdraw from them, separating our lands from theirs by means of the gallitraps. Now it is time to complete that action before they destroy us as well as themselves."

Maeve now was silent for quite some time; so long that Oberon thought that his plea might have stirred her.

"There are those," she said finally, "who contend that the Realm is linked with the mortal world; that to sunder ourselves completely from them would be to extinguish the final flickering light that now illuminates our land. That the very mortality that forces them to shine so brightly during their brief spans is food for us. What do you say to that?"

"You know who espouses that concept, as well as do I," Oberon replied contemptuously. "The scatterlings—the pariahs of both worlds. I say that their way of living proves my point. Their fascination with humanity's current ways is unhealthy—it taints them. When was the last time you admitted one of those tatterdemalions to *your* court, Queen Maeve?"

She did not appear to hear the question; once again she was silent for a time. At last she raised her gaze again to Oberon's.

"I am not prepared to take such a drastic step, Oberon. There are those of us who have more faith in humanity than you do—it is not

95

impossible that a greening of their lands might still occur. Are there not such movements among their young as might restore the old beliefs?"

"That time is past. They grow too quickly; before the ideals and bravery of human youth can have an effect, those who carry the flame are pulled down by age. Ask your scatterlings what became of those who spoke of winds of change—now they seek destruction as avidly as all the rest."

"No shit," Scott murmured. He was surprised to realize that he had become drawn into the narrative, despite its flowery and archaic style. He glanced at the mandala above the couch bed. He had never been terribly militant in the Sixties—had been too young, really, to participate in what had seemed at the time to be the inevitable revolution. *Too many of us felt that way,* he thought, *and now look at the mess we're in. Three Republican administrations in a row . . .*

Oberon was right—the idealists had grown up too quickly. He found himself remembering where he had been when he had heard the news that JFK had been shot—in the seventh grade at Trenton Junior High in New Jersey. He remembered how the teacher of the social studies class had put his head down on the desk and wept.

He shook his head, surprised at the intensity of the emotions the memory conjured. Odd that a novel about elves and fairies could trigger such feelings. He read on:

"Still," Maeve murmured, "I feel there is yet hope. The ephemerality you speak of may yet work in our favor; as long as new ones are born and believe, we can survive."

96

Oberon stared at her in disbelief. "Survive, perhaps—but is that all there is to hope for? I tell you that we can *thrive* again—that by starting over we can recapture the glory of times past! If we do not, sooner or later there will be a tragedy—of that I am sure. Humankind has proven its distrust and fear of us many times, even before they began to worship pragmatism above all other gods."

"I see no point in continuing this discussion," Maeve said. "I have told you my decision."

Oberon bowed, turned and left the hall. Only when he was far from the queen's sight, in one of the many corridors lit by smokeless torches, did he allow himself a small, rueful smile. It had gone as well as he had dared hope it might; he had planted in Maeve's thoughts the possibility of a confrontation. He had expected to accomplish no more. All that remained now was to make sure that it came to pass.

He continued on his way, past bowers of silver roses and scented pools, hearing faint notes of harps and pipes occasionally touch the air with melancholy. At last he came to stand on one of the many balconies that afforded a glimpse of the other hills so similar to the one in which they dwelled. He looked out at the misty landscape, which was as still as a painting.

His plan was the only hope of Faerie—the only chance that the Realm might prosper once more. No matter how many lives were lost, Sidhe as well as mortal man, Oberon told himself, it would be worth it.

And once the Realm was safe; when their

own sun brightened once more and they were done at last with the memories and legends that tethered them to humanity—ah, then would Faerie be a land worth ruling, and in need of a strong leader!

Oberon heard the sound of padded feet behind him, and did not turn as a large black cat leaped onto the stonework of the low wall. He stroked the cat's back as it arched against him.

"If you want it, take it—cats know that, don't they?" he murmured to the animal. "And if it is not there to be taken—why then, it must be built."

The cat purred in understanding, and Oberon raised his eyes to the distance, seeing not the grim and cheerless land before him, but the true Bright Plain of memories gone, alive with the shouts and cries of hunt and battle—and all in his honor.

Scott used an unpaid electric bill for a bookmark and put the book down on the couch beside him. He had begun his reading without great interest, and he still could not have said that he was terribly intrigued by the story. What had kept him reading were the memories conjured by the prose—and a sense of loss, surprisingly strong, centering on his past and an ephemeral world that might have been. He had never felt particularly nostalgic for the Sixties; he had been just a little too young to appreciate them fully, and, having spent his childhood in a small city in the Northeast, he had been out of the mainstream of events. Nevertheless he felt now an overwhelming wish that he had participated more, *lived* more completely in those times. The few remnants of that part of his past that he had preserved about him now, as well as, in a larger sense, these funky houseboats and the tawdry streets of such areas as Berkeley and the Haight, now seemed to him pathetic. He felt simultaneously with his desire to hang on to the past a sense of revulsion, as though he knew he was attempting to somehow reanimate something long dead.

He also felt profoundly lonely. Everything in his immediate surroundings emphasized that—his senses seemed phenomenally acute, and the wet slap of the waves against the tin-plated hull, the vaguely musty odor of long-ignored laundry and the general shabbiness of his living quarters all combined to make him very aware that he was fast approaching forty, friendless and unloved.

Scott felt a sensation at first unfamiliar—it was almost with a shock that he realized that he was crying. Not to any great degree—an uncomfortably tight throat and a dampness around his eyes were all he could manage. He took several deep breaths, unsure whether he was trying to encourage the tears or prevent them. It had the latter effect. He looked at his watch, wondering if there was anyone he could call—he desired desperately the sound of another human voice. He could think of no one. Both his parents were dead; he had no siblings; and in seven years of living in the Bay Area he had made no real friends—certainly none that he would feel comfortable or justified in calling now and speaking to of these tumultuous needs and fears.

He felt a sudden burst of empathy for Danny Thayer. Previously he had given no thought to the boy as a human being—he was at first simply a problem to be solved and later a means to an end. But now he wondered if this was how Danny felt, wherever he was—lost and alone in the great uncaring night.

He thought of Gallegher then. He had not liked her,

99

though he had felt attracted to her for a moment in the bookstore. She had been honest with him, however, had told him exactly what she wanted from him—a story, a real story for her sleazy rag of a newspaper. He found himself admiring that. He still wasn't sure if he liked her or not—he was rather more sure that she would be a disaster to get involved with, and he knew, with a certainty that was frightening, that tomorrow he would call her and ask her out.

That decision made, Scott suddenly felt unutterably weary. It was as though the decision released all the hormones in his body that triggered sleep. He didn't even unfold the couch bed, but simply stretched out on it in his clothes and pulled the blanket over him. His last coherent thought was to wonder dimly what a scatterling was.

9

The next day was clear and bright in San Francisco. Danny and Robin had not returned to the Larkspur; instead they had slept in Golden Gate Park, in a concealing nest of bushes. The bed of leaves and grass had been surprisingly warm and comfortable; Danny suspected that Robin's magic had had something to do with that, as well as protecting them from whatever urban dangers prowled the park after nightfall.

He sat up, feeling the toy ray gun in his back pocket dig into his hip as he admired the trees and flowers about him. No doubt Robin liked the park because it reminded her of Fairyland. Looking now at the carefully tended flowers and shrubbery, Danny felt surprisingly at peace, save for a small twinge of guilt for so cavalierly abandoning Roberto. But Roberto would be all right; he was a survivor.

He looked around for his new friend, but she was not in sight. The sun was high in the sky and he felt a stab of panic. Had she grown bored with him and abandoned him? Then there was a rustling in the bushes beside him, and he turned to see her grinning at him.

Danny looked at her in amazement; despite the gritty circumstances of her life, she seemed unaffected by dirt or deprivation. Her hair was still clean and combed, her face clear, her complexion radiant. Looking at her, he felt acutely aware of his own unwashed locks and body odor. It had been several days since he had had even a sponge bath in a laundromat. Knowing that she appeared as disheveled as he did to others did little to make him feel better.

His appearance did not seem to bother her, however. She pulled him to his feet exuberantly. "Come along, Keymaster! I don't know about you, but I'm hungry!"

Danny followed her along one of the park's winding paths, hurrying to keep up and abruptly aware that he was ravenous. There were so many questions he wanted to ask—about her, about the strange names she had used in reference to him, about the other scatterlings he had met yesterday—that he felt tongue-tied. Robin, seemingly able to sense his thoughts, glanced mischievously over her shoulder at him. "Have patience, Danny. Let's do things one at a time—the first being breakfast."

"Can't you just make some food—you know, like with magic?"

"I could, but like anything made of glamour, it wouldn't be very satisfying. Besides, there's food all around us"—and so saying, she pointed ahead. They were near the Japanese Tea Garden, and Danny saw a young couple with a picnic lunch arranged on a tablecloth, sitting under a blossoming cherry tree.

Danny nodded. "That's a good idea—wait till they're done and then grab what they toss," he said. Robin looked at him and shook her head as one might with a backward child. "Why settle for leftovers," she asked, "when we can have it all?"

Confused, Danny followed her to a concealed position behind the huge bronze Buddha. There she squatted on the ground, rubbing her hands together. The flickering light that he had seen her create before began to glow between her fingers, visible even in the bright sunlight. Instead of a single flickering flame, however, it seemed composed of hundreds of tiny sparks that crawled restlessly over her hands. Robin winked at him as though inviting him to share a joke, then pressed her hands flat against the ground. The sparks wriggled off and seemed to seep into the dirt. Robin stood and indicated that Danny should watch the picnicking couple.

At first nothing happened. The two, a man and a woman dressed in designer jeans and sweaters, continued to dine on fried chicken and potato salad, at one point toasting each other with bottles of beer. The breeze carried laughter and snatches of conversation to Danny. Then he noticed that the two seemed agitated. He watched as they began brushing at their clothes and the food, at first in annoyance, then frantically. They both jumped to their feet, shouting, dancing about and swatting at themselves and each other. They were too far away for Danny to hear them clearly, save for repeated cries of "Ants!"

The man tried to brush the ants away from the picnic basket, but soon gave up. At the woman's insistence he retreated, and they both hurried down one of the park paths.

Robin looked impishly proud of herself as she stood and started toward the abandoned food, pulling Danny by the hand. He hung back. "Hey, wait—I mean, I'm hungry, but not enough to eat food that's covered with ants!"

103

Robin sighed theatrically. "Danny, what *am* I going to do with you?" She had coaxed him close to the picnic area, and now she held up a chicken leg for his inspection. "Do you see any ants?"

He did not. He looked closely at the food. There was no sign of any sort of insect invasion. "*You* did that—with your magic!"

"Guilty. Shall we dine, Keymaster?"

Danny needed no further urging. He fell to with enthusiasm, devouring most of the food there. Robin, by contrast, ate fairly little. She did not touch the chicken, confining herself mostly to apples and carrot sticks. Danny offered her a wing, but she politely refused. "I need very little food, and I'm not big on eating meat."

Twenty minutes later, Danny rolled over onto his back, gloriously stuffed. "So this is how you do it—live on the street," he said. "Boy, it beats the hell out of begging. Wish I could do it."

Her expression turned serious. "You can," she said, "only you don't remember how. That's what the others and I have to teach you."

Danny was quiet for a moment. Then he said, "I always believed, deep down inside, that I had magic—that I was *different,* you know? It's like I know it's there, but I can't reach it. Sometimes it seems like I can almost remember . . . but lately when I try to it gets all mixed up with . . ." He began to shiver, though the day was uncharacteristically warm.

"Tell me," Robin said gently.

And he wanted to, he wanted to very much, he wanted to confide in her the secret terrible thing that had happened, not just once but over and over. But all he could say was, ". . . My father . . ."

"You're afraid of him." She was looking intently at

104

him, and although there was no particular sympathy in her gaze, there was no accusation either—only an enormous desire to understand.

"I . . . ran away from him. I won't ever go back. If he ever finds me . . ." he swallowed dryly. The fear was an overpowering, hammering thing.

"He won't," Robin assured him. "Not where you are going."

"If you can teach me how to . . ." He hesitated, unable to express in words the intensity of hope and fear that the possibility engendered in him.

Robin nodded. "It won't be easy. But we'll try to teach you. All of us will try."

AFTER THEY FINISHED THEIR meal they wandered through the park for a time, looking at the conservatory of flowers and the museums. They eventually exited at the intersection of Haight and Stanyan. The street and the edge of the park here were filled, as usual, with a colorful and heterogeneous collection of street people, derelicts and teenagers. Street musicians played steel drums and guitars, other folk juggled sticks or played hackesack. It was a familiar scene to Danny; he had hung out here more than once hitting up the yuppies who braved the crowd to reach the sushi bars and shops farther down the street.

He recognized several street people. He saw Iron Jack, an old vet who suffered from a nerve disorder caused by Agent Orange. He rode the sidewalks in a motorized wheelchair, and was quite good at handling it.

"Hey, Iron Jack!"

The older man grinned a gap-toothed smile at Danny when he recognized the boy. "You seen Shanti around?" Iron Jack asked.

105

So much had happened in the past few days that Danny had forgotten giving Shanti the spellstone on Broadway when she had been driven away in the BMW. He felt a flash of worry as he shook his head, but suppressed it. Shanti knew what the dangers were on the streets. He wasn't responsible for her.

He bid Iron Jack farewell and left the shaggy-haired ex-soldier spinning his wheelchair like a mechanized dervish, cackling madly as he did so. He rejoined Robin, following her as she made her way through the gathering throng at the edge of the park, past a row of ghetto blasters that provided pounding rap music and to a small group dressed in archaic Sixties-style clothes who stood somewhat apart from the main body of the crowd.

Danny recognized them as the same ones they had met in the tree grove on Telegraph Hill. This was the first time he had seen them clearly; there were five of them, all as ageless in appearance as Robin. He remembered that the one with the patched jeans and the top hat was called Patch, and that Puck wore dark clothes and sunglasses. Robin introduced him now to the rest: a compact fellow wearing a fringed buckskin jacket was Pinch, the girl in the miniskirt and beads was Lull, and a tall, angular boy wearing a tattered opera cloak was Random.

They seemed no warmer toward Danny than they had been the last time they met, regarding him with cool expressions. "Does he remember anything more?" Pinch asked Robin.

"Not so far. If we take him to a gallitrap, maybe that will jog his memory."

"Hey," Danny said, "stop talking about me like I'm not here, okay? After all, if I'm who you say I am, then I oughtta be pretty important to you guys."

"A round-ears asking for respect," Patch said with amusement. "I love it."

"He deserves it," Robin said; for the first time since Danny had met her there was a hint of asperity in her tone. "Let's go; the sooner we reach the gate, the sooner we might all be able to go home."

Danny's breath began to quicken at this, whether from excitement or fear not even he could tell. To hear Robin tell it, it might be only a matter of hours, or even less, before he entered Fairyland! The other scatterlings did not seem to be overly excited about the prospect, and he suspected this was because they did not believe that he could really do whatever he was supposed to do to make it happen. Well, he would show them! He would make Robin proud of him—

"Trouble," Lull said in a low voice. Danny turned and saw several young men, appearing to be in their late teens or early twenties, coming toward them. They were wearing boots, torn jeans and nylon bomber jackets. Their hair was cut so short as to render them nearly bald, and they had tattoos of snakes and swastikas on their arms. *Oh shit,* Danny thought, feeling his stomach roil with sudden dread. *Skinheads.*

He looked about. They were far enough from the others in the park that the neo-Nazis would feel they could safely indulge in a quick bit of violence before anyone might try to stop them. Danny turned to run—that was the only reaction that offered even a hope of survival when confronted by such thugs. Before he could do so, however, Robin laid her hand lightly across his upper arm, and he found he could no more move than if he were chained to her. He watched helplessly as the skinheads approached.

The one who was apparently their leader stopped a few feet away, put his hands on his hips and surveyed them. He was thin, and though he was not a body-builder like Roberto, his arms were hard with ropelike muscles. A sneer seemed perpetually engraved on his face. Danny noticed the tattoo of an eagle on the back of his right hand.

"Looka this," he said, his tone dripping scorn. "What time machine did *you* dickheads crawl out of?"

"I seen 'em around here before, Jake," another skinhead with a spider tattooed on his bald scalp said. "They think this is still the fuckin' Summer of Love."

They were edging closer—preparing to strike, Danny knew. They carried no weapons that he could see, but he knew how much damage they could inflict with their fists and their steel-toed boots. He glanced at the scatterlings. They did not seem afraid; in fact, Robin and Puck were smiling slightly. Robin raised a hand and pointed behind the skinheads. "Company's coming," she said.

The one called Jake did not turn around. Two of his subordinates did, however, and reacted uneasily. Danny looked past them to where Robin was pointing. He could see nothing save two old winos shambling in their general direction, both obviously too drunk to appreciate the danger they were approaching.

One of the skinheads grabbed Jake's shoulder. "Hey, we better boogie, man." Jake turned and looked at the winos, then back at Danny and the scatterlings. Danny could see hatred and exasperation in his expression. Danny looked back, expecting to see the winos. But they were gone; in their place were two very stern-looking cops bearing down on them.

Jake hesitated, then said truculently, "Hey, we'll be around." The skinheads moved off toward the street, becoming lost in the crowd after a few moments.

108

Danny breathed a sigh of relief. "Boy, you guys know all kinds of tricks, don't you?"

"Enough to survive," Puck said. "And now it's time we taught you a trick or two. Come along, Danny. Let's see what the sight of a gallitrap does for you."

DOUGLAS CRAIG HAD NOT slept for the rest of that long, surreal night. Now, sitting and staring at the midday sun's glitter on the bay, he wondered almost seriously if he would ever sleep again.

He turned and faced the blown-up photograph that hung on the south wall of his study. He thought back to that long-ago night in the Muir Woods, of that single glimpse of another world, caught for better or worse—he had never been sure—on film. He remembered feeling the tiny, insistent tugging of the sprites that flickered about him, hearing their laughter as they urged him toward the glowing opening. He had held back, had lost his opportunity. And had regretted it ever since.

Why? he wondered. *Why did I desire so much to walk the fields of Faerie?*

He could understand his longing for it now, after a broken marriage, a ruined career, a wasted life. But back then he had had everything going for him. He had been one of the most sought-after photographic artists in the country. He could travel on assignment anywhere on Earth as long as he brought back his unique vision of those places. His wife and daughter had admired and adored him. He had been young, in good health . . .

And he had been unsatisfied. Not one of all those pictures he had taken had been what he wanted it to be. He was given to understand that most artists, whatever their medium, have this complaint—the writer looks at his published works and complains that these are not the

109

right words; the way the composer hears his piece played cannot compare with the way he heard it in his head. Craig had tried to accept that as a fact of life, but he had not been able to do so. He had always kept looking for that one shot that would be everything he wanted it to be.

And beyond the swirling motes of the gallitrap, he had seen it—just as he saw it now, hanging on the wall before him. It had survived the quake of '89 when all the others on the wall had crashed to the floor—almost as if it were somehow charmed. The one shot with which he was totally satisfied. The only one.

Beyond that swirling ring had been a world full of perfect vistas. If a special heaven had been reserved for artists, than surely he had seen it—and lost his chance to travel among its lands.

But now, maybe, just maybe, he would have another chance. For it was now obvious that fairies did still walk among humankind. But how was he to find them? And how to convince them to take him where he wanted to go?

Craig turned away from the picture. He had not had a drink since he had left that last bar—he was uncharacteristically sober for this time of day. Well, that at least was something he could fix.

He started toward the bar, then suddenly stopped. Something had occurred to him that he had not seriously thought about in a long time—the possibility that now might not be the time for a drink.

"If I drink," he said aloud in a musing tone, "then this second chance will go the way of the first one. And do I really want that to happen?"

The lure of the liquor was very strong, however—almost a physical attraction, as if the bottles were an array of magnets and he a helpless iron filing. It required conscious effort to turn away. He knew he would not be

110

able to resist drinking if he remained in the house. He would take a walk, clear his head, give himself some time to think . . .

Besides, there was always the possibility of coming across a new tavern.

Craig left his mansion and walked briskly down North Point.

10

Scott splurged on a taxi from the ferry to the Sunset district where Gallegher lived. He was surprised at how nervous he was about the upcoming date as the cab weaved through the park. It had not been easy to call her and ask her out—he had fully expected her to laugh and tell him no. But she had not; instead, after only a moment's hesitation she had agreed. To his own disgust Scott realized that his first reaction had not been pleasure, but rather suspicion of any ulterior motives she might have for agreeing to go out with him.

She lived in a third-floor walkup facing the park. The cramped lobby was littered with old neighborhood newspapers and flyers, and the stairwell smelled faintly of mildew. Scott was mildly shocked—somehow he thought she would be living in a nicer place, though upon reflection he realized that she couldn't be making all that much money at her job.

When he knocked on the door she opened it and slipped out, and Scott glimpsed clothes hanging on doorknobs and over the backs of chairs, and Chinese takeout containers littering a couch and coffee table. She evidently did not want him to know that she was sloppy, but was unwilling to clean it up and invite him in. He almost smiled.

She stood on the landing, looking at him with an expression that seemed half wary and half amused. She was wearing a blue shift and a coat, and no jewelry. Even so, Russell felt shabby next to her in his jeans and corduroy jacket. "So, where shall we eat?" she asked.

"How about Chinese?" He felt pleased with himself for suggesting it. He knew she liked it from the brief view he had had of her apartment, and cheap Chinese restaurants were always plentiful in the city.

"Had it last night. How about sushi? There's a place not far from here that's fairly cheap." She started down the stairs without waiting for an answer. Scott followed, telling himself that her take-charge attitude was something to be appreciated rather than annoyed with.

Both were silent as they walked through the cold night air. Fog was moving in from the direction of Mount Sutro; Scott caught glimpses as he walked of the huge tower that loomed above the drifting mist like a Martian war machine, its red lights blinking.

Gallegher moved like a woman on a mission; he had to stretch his legs to keep up with her. "What's your hurry? The night is young."

"Yeah, but I'm hungry."

He said, "I read your article." He hadn't intended to bring it up until dinner or even after, but he couldn't help it—the silence between them was making him uncomfortable, even though they'd only been together a few moments.

114

Gallegher did not slow her pace or look at him. "Good."

So much for that conversational gambit. "Yeah, well—I liked it."

"Let me guess—you think it shows promise, and you want to know why I'm working for a rag like the *Star.*"

Scott stopped; Gallegher walked a few steps farther before realizing she was alone. She looked back at him.

"Right now, all I want to know is two things," he said. "One: what in God's name possessed me to call you for a date, and two: what in God's name possessed you to say 'yes.'"

She looked at him silently for a long moment, her face half-shadowed by the light of a street lamp in what he couldn't help thinking of as classic *film noir* style. Then she sighed and walked back to him. "I'm sorry," she said. "I won't tell you it's been a bitch of a day, or that I've got my period, or any of the other traditional excuses. But I *am* sorry. I'll try to be a little easier to get along with. Now c'mon—let's have dinner."

It was more than he had expected by way of apology, and he wisely forbore to comment on it. They walked without speaking the remaining two blocks to the restaurant, but it was a much more comfortable silence now. Scott thought that the evening just might work out all right after all. There was only one more hurdle to cross in the immediate future, and that was his deep and abiding distrust of sushi and those who ate it.

LIZ WATCHED WITH AMUSEMENT as Russell looked doubtfully at the menu. "You do like Japanese food, I hope."

"Well, yeah—stuff like teriyaki and tempura. Raw fish, though . . ."

"Sushi isn't just raw fish." She plucked the menu from his hand. "May I?" As if on cue the waitress was there, pen poised over order pad. Liz ordered the usual safe items for a new initiate: *ebi,* crab roll, *futomaki* and the ubiquitous California roll. For herself she included a tuna hand roll, sea eel and salmon *sashimi.* She ordered Kirin and Russell asked for mineral water. As she handed the menus to the waitress, she saw Russell sharpening his wooden chopsticks by rubbing them against each other. Thank God he wasn't a complete stranger to ethnic food.

She really wasn't sure why she had decided to go out with him. There was the obvious reason, of course, that of learning more about the intriguing case of Danny Thayer. Was that all there was to it? She didn't know. She supposed part of it was curiosity—she had not expected him to call, and there was a certain amount of interest engendered by his doing so. But there had to be more to it than that—curiosity certainly didn't drive her to date every clown who called her.

Liz watched him as he glanced about the place, taking it in. That was something she found charming about men: put them in a new place and they were always curious, like cats. Women were usually reluctant to show so much obvious interest in their surroundings. The waitress came with bowls of miso soup, and Russell sipped at his. Liz noticed his hands; they had long fingers and clean nails and knuckles. She liked that also. He was not wearing rings, which was another point in his favor; she had never been able to get used to jewelry on men, even gay men. Thank God he didn't have a pierced ear.

He looked at her. His eyes were clear, not muddy or bloodshot, but a bit too close-set for her taste. "Did you read the book?" he asked.

116

"The fantasy? No. Haven't had time. I read the comic, though." She made a dismissive gesture.

He ran a hand through his hair, which was red and thinning. Normally Liz didn't like pattern baldness, but Russell's suited him somehow. "I can see the appeal of that stuff," he said. "Particularly to someone who might not be all that happy with real life."

"You mean like most of the *Star*'s readers."

He ignored that. "I can also see how easy it can be for people to believe it—I mean believe *in* it. I had an aunt once who was addicted to soap operas. She was convinced that they were real—that her TV was like a magic window on these people's lives."

The sushi tray arrived at this point. Russell eyed it dubiously. Liz took charge, pouring the soy sauce and mixing a small amount of *wasabi* in it. She picked up a California roll and dipped it in the sauce, then offered it to the detective. "Try it. Your mouth will love you."

He took it. "Aren't you supposed to use chopsticks?"

"Your choice. I find the little buggers tend to fall apart when I do." She picked up a sliver of eel on its cushion of rice and took a bite. Heaven.

Russell hesitated, then took a deep breath and popped the delicacy into his mouth. He chewed tentatively, then with gusto. "Not bad. In fact, it's pretty good." The relief was evident in his voice.

"Another convert." They ate in silence for a few minutes before Liz said, "You're not exactly the popular image of a detective."

Russell grinned wryly. "Don't I know it. Believe me, you're not the only one who's said that."

"I'm trying to visualize you in a seedy office down past Market, with your name lettered on the glass of the door. It isn't easy."

117

"I don't have an office. Actually, I only became a 'private' detective a few days ago. Until then I was an operative for a detective agency."

"You quit to go into business for yourself?"

"Not exactly. I was fired. You see—" He stopped, looked straight at her and said, "The truth is, I'm a lousy detective. I couldn't find my ass with a geiger counter and radioactive suppositories."

Liz nearly sprayed a mouthful of beer on the tablecloth. "Excuse me for laughing—I didn't think you had a sense of humor."

"At times. Not often, anymore."

"The next inevitable question is: Why are you doing this if you're no good at it?"

She realized as she asked it that she was requesting his life story. Fortunately he was considerate enough to give her the abridged version. And one part of it actually impressed her. "Edward Thayer! You really know him?"

"I did, a long time ago. Don't tell me you do too?"

"I've seen some of the movies he's produced. *The Point of No Return,* with Jeff Bridges, was very good." She nibbled at another piece of sushi. "So you're trying to find his son. That makes any story I could get out of this worth quite a bit more."

"I don't want this case trivialized or sensationalized," he said slowly. "Certainly not until I've either found the boy or given up, and preferably not afterward."

"Then why tell me your life story, Russell? If you think it'll get me in bed with you, the answer is probably not. If you think it'll get you sympathy, well, maybe, but that's not going to do you much good."

"I would love to go to bed with you," he said—the frankness of his admission kept her from making a comeback remark. "But don't take it personally. Just about every woman I see who's the least bit attractive I want to go to bed with. I'm lonely, I'm not exactly a success, and I'm having a dandy mid-life crisis right now. So, yeah, I'm probably unburdening myself to you for those reasons and more. If it's boring, I apologize. I called you because I read part of that book the woman sold us, and I realized in reading it that maybe we—I mean all of us, the human race—maybe we had something once, about twenty years ago, that could have been"—he groped aimlessly in the air—"I don't know, *life*—instead of the lousy plastic imitation that we've got now. We fucked up. All of us. Even the ones who thought they kept fighting. I don't just mean bigger bombs and more acid rain and the greenhouse effect . . . I mean that there was a moment when we could have been what we wanted to be. You. Me. All of us." He hesitated as if about to say more, then shook his head and took a long swig of his Perrier as though he wished it were alcoholic.

Liz ate another piece of sushi while she considered this outburst. Part of her—*be honest,* she told herself, *a large part of you*—was tempted to respond with a cynical retort about aging hippiethink and the sporadic attempts to revivify the moldering corpse of the Sixties. But she had to be honest—his little speech was touching, and she wasn't sure how to respond to it. She remembered her own sense of activism and idealism in those days. She had been only thirteen years old in 1969, but she still recalled vividly the sense of outrage she had felt at the Kent State shootings. She had, in fact, always regretted to a small degree having just missed that celebrated decade—by the time she had been old enough to visit the Haight, its glory had faded considerably. True, there were still old hippies to be seen, like endangered species on an animal preserve, and there were even young kids, born ten years

119

after the Summer of Love, now strutting around in tie-dyed shirts and buckskin vests, lugging twelve-string guitars. But it wasn't the same. It would never be the same.

"I was at Woodstock," Russell said abruptly.

Liz looked at him skeptically. "Really? I mean, if everyone who said they were at Woodstock had really been at Woodstock, I think the entire Atlantic seaboard would've collapsed under the weight."

He smiled. "No, really. A bunch of friends of mine and I ditched school in Albany. We got there about two days into it. We had to walk about fifteen miles through the mud from where we parked. We never got closer than a mile to the stage. There were more people than I've ever seen in one place in my life, and lots of them were naked. It's a wonderful nostalgic thing for people to look back on now, but at the time I remember being appalled at the garbage and the unsanitary conditions. I ate a hamburger at a tent cookout and got the runs. And the music—half the time we couldn't hear it, and the other half of the time the feedback would nearly melt your brain. But I was there. Sometimes I think it's the one exciting thing I've done in my life." He ate another piece of sushi, then said, "This kid, Danny—I've got to find him. I think it's more than a job now."

JAKE CALVIN HAD ATTENDED his first meeting of the Aryan Apostles when he was sixteen, and he had been going back sporadically for the last three years. There were times when he believed fervently in the supremacy of the white Anglo-Saxon race and its God-given right and duty to drive all inferior races and bloods from the shores of America. There were other times when he simply enjoyed the camaraderie and the opportunities to do some serious stomping on fags and other human refuse with which the streets of San Francisco were overflowing.

Tonight was another night to do something about it, to make an effort, no matter how small, to keep his country untainted. Tonight Jake had a plan.

He walked down Haight Street alone. He had said nothing to his fellows about what he intended to do. He considered himself a man of action, not of words. His actions, after all, were what had given him the leadership of the local chapter of the Apostles. He was only nineteen, but he had already been in family court and juvenile detention five times for such charges as attempted rape and sexual abuse, possession of drugs and weapons, dealing and attempted murder. He had done more than attempt the latter, but those crimes had gone unnoticed. It was so easy to kill someone.

Even his family feared him—had, in fact, fled from him. The last time he got out of detention they had moved from the tiny apartment he had grown up in, with no forwarding address.

He swaggered through the door of a video arcade. The bouncer saw him, gave him the eye, and Jake made a pacifying gesture. He wasn't looking for trouble this night. Not yet, anyway.

He looked around. Over half the machines had players feeding quarters and destroying spaceships or devouring animated blips. Jake wended his way through the maze of arcade games to a small door in the back marked EMPLOYEES ONLY. The door had a peephole with a fisheye lens above the sign. Behind the door and past a large man with cold eyes was a flight of stairs, and at the top of the stairs other types of games were being played.

It was here that Jake knew he would find the Rock.

He was right, of course; the big biker was sitting with several of his cohorts on a grimy unfolded futon in the

121

dimly lit room, cranked to the gills, staring at a television in the corner that was showing MTV with the sound off. Jake stood in front of the Rock and waited for him to focus, then said, "I need some artillery."

The Rock's response was predictable. "What the fuck you talkin' about, asshole?"

Jake squatted down next to the Rock, dug his fingers into the filthy beard and pulled the biker's face toward him. The Rock was too surprised, and too stoned, to protest. "I need guns," Jake continued softly. "Everybody knows you got connections out at the Presidio."

He released the Rock's beard and sat back on his heels, smiling. The room had gotten very quiet; everyone who could track what was going on was waiting for violence to start. Jake was waiting for it too; still crouched, he balanced lightly on the balls of his feet, ready to shoot straight up and back if necessary, one hand hovering near the shiv at his ankle. The tension of the moment rushed through him like a line of coke. He took a deep breath, smelling the fumes of sinsemilla and Jamaican. At that moment, more than anything else, he wanted the biker to go for him.

The Rock rubbed his beard meditatively, then squinted red-rimmed eyes at Jake. "You run that buncha skins hangs out in the Haight, don'tcha?"

Jake nodded.

"I heard about you." He thought for a moment, then said, "I got a buncha forty-fives they're shipping out; been replaced by Berettas."

Jake grinned and stood up. "Pleasure doing business with you," he said, and walked out, aware of the bikers' gaze on his back, knowing that once again the superior will of his pure bloodline had cowed his inferiors into serving his purpose. It was a good feeling.

11

Danny soon realized that, like Robin, the rest of the scatterlings were neither highly organized nor motivated. Though they talked longingly of returning to the gallitrap, whatever that was, they were quite easily turned from their purpose by all manner of distractions. After the incident with the skinheads they spent some time wandering about the Haight, pointing out to each other wall murals and colorfully painted Victorians. Eventually they caught a bus, magically distracting the driver and passengers from the fact that they did not pay, and rode north through Pacific Heights, disembarking near the Palace of Fine Arts. More aimless wandering through the rotunda and about the pond followed. The way they exclaimed in wonder at the columns and statues, Danny would have sworn they had never seen them before, though Robin assured him that this was one of their favorite haunts. The scatterlings were very like children in their constant delight and fascination with the world.

An impromptu tour of the Exploratorium followed.

This Danny rather enjoyed as well, since he had never been in the huge hands-on science fair. Once again no one seemed to notice that they entered without paying. Danny began to lose himself in the spirit of things. It was easy to get caught up in the scatterlings' lackadaisical attitude; after all, their philosophy of taking life moment by moment was quite similar to his own. When they grew hungry, they ate: vending machines disgorged food and drink for them without demanding payment. Provender and entertainment were theirs for the taking; what more could one ask?

Also, Danny was coming to realize that as long as he was with Robin he was happy, no matter if they were in this world or another. His infatuation with her was not sexual—sex and love were two very different things to him—but no less consuming for that. As the group wandered through the cavernous interior of the building, peering through a huge lens that made the entire room seem upside down or crawling through the dark closeness of the Tactile Dome, Danny contrived always to be near her.

He tried to question her more about the mysterious task the scatterlings had for him, but it was difficult to carry on a conversation because Robin was constantly being distracted by her desire to manipulate various exhibits. Eventually, however, she came to a stop at a huge glass cylinder in which bolts of colored lightning flashed and crackled. The two of them stood beside it, tracing their fingertips lightly over the glass and watching the writhing arcs of energy following their hands.

"You're a princess, aren't you?" he asked her.

She looked at him incredulously. "What gives you that idea?"

He fumbled for words, suddenly uncertain. "Well . . .

124

I mean, you're so beautiful, and . . . in the stories there's always a princess who's been exiled from her kingdom . . ."

She started to laugh, but then stopped and looked at him. There was an uncharacteristic tenderness in her usually mercurial eyes, in which he could see reflected the shifting hues of the glass tube. "Danny," she said, "you must understand that your tales of magic and heroism don't apply here. Faerie is as real as this world, and just as dangerous in its own way. Both of us—all of us"—and she gestured at the other scatterlings absorbed with the exhibits all about them—"are just trying to get home. I'm not a princess—but if you can do what I think you can, then you might well be a hero—at least, to us."

"But *what* do you want me to do? And what if I don't know how?"

She looked at his hands, which were nervously stroking the blown glass between them. The vivid discharges followed his movements, for what reason he could not fathom. "You can make the lightning follow your hand," she said. "Do you know why?"

Danny shook his head.

"It doesn't matter. All that matters is that you can do it. Now watch." Robin gestured for him to remove his hands from the tube, which he did. Then she began to move her hands over the glass, not touching it, weaving her fingers in strange cabalistic patterns. Danny realized with a tingle of excitement that she was making magic.

The discharges in the cylinder began to shift in response to her hands' movements. Instead of restlessly hurling itself against the inside of the glass, the electrical energy began to curl back upon itself, shifting and roiling near the center. The various colors deepened. The lightning formed into a crackling oval, surrounding darkness. Danny stared into it. Deep within the black center, tiny motes of light moved. Danny watched, enraptured, as the darkness seemed to expand, drawing him in—the gleaming center rushed toward him as though he were falling down an endless well toward something . . .

Something wonderful . . .

Danny felt himself pull back physically, as though attempting to stop himself from plunging headlong into some unknowable abyss. He blinked and stared at the glass cylinder, in which the lightning flashed as it had before Robin had cast her spell. He looked at her, aware somehow that he had been shown something of vast importance, but still unsure what it was. Robin's inscrutable expression gave him no clue.

Before he could ask her about what she had just showed him, the scatterling turned away toward her companions. "We've wasted enough time," she said. "Let's do it."

Though she spoke barely loud enough for him to hear, Patch, Lull, Puck and the others immediately stopped their various activities and converged on them. "You still think he can pull this off?" Patch said, watching Danny with open contempt.

"Ease up, Patch," Random said. "If we don't give it a shot, we'll never know. And we've got to go back. If we stay here, we'll—"

Patch turned and looked at him, and though he was smaller than Random it was the latter who flinched back. "We'll what? Die? You don't *know* that. None of us know for sure. What's there for us under the hill, anyway? No better treatment, that's for sure. At least here we've got an advantage." He snapped his fingers and a blue spark of flame leaped up, startling Danny.

"Enough arguing," Robin said. "The majority rules, Patch. You know that."

126

Patch shrugged. "So which one? North Beach, or Muir Woods, or—"

Robin shook her head. "The cables."

A moment of silence followed her statement. Danny got the distinct feeling that the others were surprised, even shocked. "North Beach is closer," Lull pointed out.

"Too much chance of being seen," Puck said. "We can't distract everyone who comes in the store while we're working on the gallitrap. Robin's right—it has to be the cables."

Patch shrugged. "Okay. Then if we're going to do it, let's do it."

DANNY WAS SURPRISED TO realize that they had spent most of the day in the Exploratorium—shadows were growing longer and fog was drifting through the streets. The group made its way quickly over to Hyde Street, where they caught the southbound cable car to Jackson. Their destination was the Cable Car Museum, an imposing two-story structure at the corner of Mason and Washington. Danny had never seen it before. It was after hours and the building was closed, but that did not stop the scatterlings—the door yielded to Puck's touch as easily as if he had put a key into the lock.

Inside was even more impressive than outside. The interior was filled with huge machines, massive turning wheels and gears that guided the cables through their endless route. The sounds of the machinery were not loud, but they suggested great power to Danny. He leaned over the railing, staring in fascination at the apparatus. These machines weren't like computers or TVs, which worked by their own kind of magic—you could *see* how these things operated, just like the devices at the Exploratorium.

127

The scatterlings, however, did not seem nearly as interested in what drove the cable cars. They hustled Danny past the gift stand and down a flight of stairs into the lower depths of the building.

The stairs ended in a large concrete chamber. Danny marveled at the huge gothic arches and I-beams that supported the ceiling. Ladder rungs in a wall led down into another chamber through which the cables ran, whipping around huge angled wheels that spun endlessly. "Follow us," Robin said to Danny, speaking loudly over the high-pitched whine of the machinery. "And be careful— the iron threads on those cables can take your skin right off."

Danny followed them down the ladder and into the room. It was surprisingly warm. Pipes overhead vented steam, and there were a few rusted oil drums stacked against the wall; other than that, the room was empty save for the heavy cables that hummed by much too close for comfort. His shoes crunched on delicate shards of metal that had peeled from the thick strands over the years. A single electric bulb in the ceiling relieved the darkness somewhat, but Danny still felt like he was in a dank and gloomy dungeon beneath some evil king's castle. Under other circumstances—had he, for example, stumbled upon this location by himself—he would have been quite happy to have found a place so ideally suited to his fantasy excursions. Now, however, he was too overwhelmed with all that had happened in the past two days, and too concerned with accomplishing whatever task the scatterlings desired him to do.

They edged carefully around the madly spinning wheels. At one point a rat scurried across the tunnel floor and into a crack in the wall; Danny nearly stepped on it. He remembered reading a comic book recently that had

128

to do with subterranean creatures living beneath the streets of New York City in miles and miles of tunnels, storm drains, subways and the like that connected into a vast and complex warren, forming an underground city in its own right. He wondered if the same were true for San Francisco. The thought was both intriguing and frightening.

While he was engaged in these thoughts, he realized that the others were looking at him expectantly. Danny glanced from one to another of them, then fixed his gaze on Robin. He could see the barest suggestion of disappointment in her expression, as though he had failed some obscure test. She said, "Does this place seem familiar to you, Keymaster?"

"Why should it?" he asked sullenly. He was tired of this. These scatterlings were as bad as parents and teachers, always expecting, demanding, more than he could give. He suddenly wished he had never laid eyes upon Robin, but even as he silently expressed the thought he knew that it wasn't true.

"It is one of the gallitraps," Robin replied quietly. "A hinge between the worlds."

"So what? You still ain't told me what I'm supposed to *do*!"

Robin's voice was quieter still when she replied; he could barely hear her over the whine of the cables' endless journey.

"Open it," she said.

Danny stared at her and the others in perplexed resentment. Open *what*? He looked around; other than the way they came in, there were no doors in the walls and no access in the floor or ceiling.

"I *told* you, " Patch said.

"Let's not give up yet," Puck replied. He stepped

closer to Danny, his eyes invisible behind the sunglasses that he wore even in this gloom. "Danny," he said intensely, "reach into yourself. Feel the magic that lives inside you. I know it's there; you know it's there. Draw it out, let it go—*use* it. It's as easy as breathing."

Danny stared from one to another of the scatterlings, trying to keep the panic he felt under control. It was the same sick, helpless feeling he remembered so well when confronted by his father; the knowledge that he had done *something* wrong, though he never knew exactly what; the surety that he was a *bad boy* who had to be punished, perhaps by the belt, or the flat of his father's big heavy hands, or worse (so much worse), the pain of the *other thing*— ·

He realized he was shivering. He shut his eyes in desperation, retreating within himself the same way he always did when the *other thing* was going on, denying the hurt, the humiliation, seeing that bright core of magic that he knew lived deep inside himself. Danny sought it now, reaching for it as though it were a lifeline. And, oddly, it seemed this time as though the magic within himself was also a door, a door that led from his heart into a world as vast as his imagination. It was there, waiting to be opened, had he but the key.

But this time his magic eluded him, seemed to slip through the questing fingers of his desire. As if from a great distance he heard Robin saying, "You're trying too hard! Relax, just let it happen!" But he couldn't. The warm, comforting light that he had filled himself with so often before, the light that blinded him and filled his sensations, damping the agony of what his father was doing to him, faded, as it had sometimes happened before, leaving him defenseless against the brutality, only ashes within his heart.

130

Defeated, Danny opened his eyes. He caught the merest glimpse of what seemed to be a light in the dim tunnel—purer and more golden by far than the tawdry illumination of the electric bulb. But it was gone the instant he saw it, leaving only a fading afterimage—that, and a single breath of air sweeter than any he had ever tasted before.

He did not know what had happened—he only knew that he had failed, and the knowledge of that was almost too much shame to be borne. Danny turned to Robin, putting his face against her shoulder, trying desperately not to cry.

"You see?" he heard Patch say. "I knew he didn't have it."

"He did, for a moment," Puck's quiet voice replied. "The power is there. We just have to teach him how."

"We'd better hurry," Lull pointed out. "It'll be Walpurgis Night soon. If we don't get the gallitrap open by then . . ."

"We will," Robin said. Her voice sounded deep and comforting, coming as much from her body as her lips, and it stirred in Danny a vague memory of the touch of soft hands and a soothing maternal voice. "He'll remember how."

"What makes you think so?" Patch's tone was challenging. "You thought showing him the gallitrap would work, and it didn't. What else can we try?"

Robin looked at Danny for a long minute before replying. "We'll think of something," she said.

The music reached a final discordant crescendo and stopped, leaving the thick blue air still vibrating. "Stupid fuckin' stage divers," Spike mumbled. He and Thomas were sitting at the table with Jake, drinking cheap wine out of paper bags in deference to the club's lack of a liquor license. "Had one land on my table once, man. Broke a bottle on his fuckin' head." He laughed at the memory. He wiped sweat from his bald head, which was tattooed with a large swastika.

"Band's getting old," Thomas said. "They been here, what—two years? Fuckin' Grateful Dead."

"I like them," Jake said softly. Thomas took a long swig out of his bag and looked uncomfortable.

A shadow fell over the table then, blocking the flickering light from the overhead fluorescents. Jake looked up to see the Rock looming over him. "Hey, Rock," he said with an easy smile. "What's news?"

"It's all set up," the biker told him. "We'll meet you at three tomorrow morning outside Nate's. You got the cash, you get the artillery. You jackin' us off"—the Rock gave him a yellow grin—"you get a hog ride right up your ass, tough boy."

Jake was no longer smiling. He said nothing further, but simply looked at the big man, his eyes like shadows. The Rock turned abruptly and left, pushing his way roughly through the crowd.

Spike said trepidatiously, "You ain't been talking much about this, Jake. What's this gun shit about?"

Jake grinned, tracing with one fingernail the burn patterns and drink stains on the table. "We're gonna do it to those assholes we saw in the park yesterday."

Spike and Thomas looked at each other. "What for?" Thomas asked.

12

Jake and his two lieutenants, Spike and Thomas, wer[e]
sitting in a club in the Soma district. A local speed-meta[l]
band, White Noise, was playing. The volume made conversation impossible; all one could do was sit and let the
sound, which battered the air hard enough to leave the
skin tingling, assault one.

It was Friday night, and the small basement room was
packed. Teenagers festooned with leather and meta[l]
studs, some with hair moussed to over a foot above their
heads, jostled and slammed against each other in response to the music. One skinny girl, perhaps fourteen—i[t]
was hard to judge someone's age, Jake thought, with most
of their hair shaved off—climbed onto the stage and tried
to grab the lead singer. He pushed her away; she half fell,
half dove off the stage, landing in a knot of her friends.
Jake noticed that her nose and ear were bleeding; she had
been wearing a chain connecting a nosering to an earring
and both had been torn out during the fall. She staggered
to her feet, laughing.

"They look like foreigners to me," Jake replied. "There's something weird about them."

"So we find 'em and stomp 'em," Spike said. "But shooting 'em is kind of serious, ain't it?"

Before Jake could reply, the band started another set, rendering conversation impossible again. He stood, gesturing to his lieutenants to follow him, and made his way to the door.

Outside, the cold, clean night air was almost enough to make him dizzy. He walked quickly, taking long strides, forcing his two cohorts to hurry to keep up. The street they were on was lined with dark warehouses, interspersed with occasional trendy boutiques and restaurants. The sidewalks were blocked by overflowing dumpsters. A thrasher on a skateboard sailed past them at high speed.

"Hey, Jake, c'mon," said Spike, "y'gonna answer me or not?"

"Yeah," Thomas ventured boldly, "I don't think we need to hit 'em. We just kick their asses, show 'em they ain't welcome—"

They were passing one of the boutiques; its name was inscribed in Art Deco neon, blinking on and off on the wall. Jake suddenly turned and grabbed Thomas, twisting both fists into the lapels of the latter's jacket and pulling Thomas's face close to his own. "You want to run things, Thomas?" he asked softly.

Thomas's face was ashen even in the ruddy glow of the sign next to them. He shook his head quickly. "No, Jake, no, c'mon, I was just makin' a suggestion . . ."

"I want your advice, I'll fucking well ask for it!" Jake lifted Thomas from the sidewalk and smashed him back against the pulsing tubing of the sign. The thin glass shattered into powder, surrounding them with shadows.

135

Jake let Thomas fall to the pavement and turned away. Spike helped Thomas to his feet, and the two of them hurried after Jake, Thomas picking slivers of glass from his neck. Behind them they could hear the owner of the boutique shouting for the police.

LIZ STOPPED OUTSIDE THE door of her apartment building and smiled at Scott, feeling oddly shy. The dinner conversation had been far better than she had thought it would be. Both of them were slightly tipsy; she had talked Scott into a couple of cups of saki.

Now he stood before her, hands thrust into the pockets of his coat, looking uncomfortable. Liz sighed. "The inevitable awkward moment on every first date," she said. "To invite him up or not? In this case, I'm afraid it's 'not.' I've got to be up early tomorrow."

He nodded, not seeming too disappointed—and she noticed, to her surprise, a disappointment of her own at that. "I understand. Same here. Tomorrow I have to do some job hunting in addition to looking for Danny."

Liz hesitated, then said gently, "The chances of finding him really are pretty slim, Scott. You need to know that, if you don't already. After a few weeks, they just disappear. Most of them use street names, so there's practically no way to trace them."

He examined the sidewalk between his shoes. "You sound like you know something about this."

"Just because I make up newspaper stories about the mean streets doesn't mean I don't know what goes on out there for real. He may not even be alive by now. Something like ninety percent of the kids on the streets will experience violence in some form or other. They sell themselves or others sell them. For a couple of grand you can buy a kid, boy or girl, as young as you want, to be your slave."

136

"When I first took this job," he said softly, "I thought it was a godsend. A way to pry myself out of debt and hang on until I could find steady employment. I really didn't give much thought about Danny—he was just a means to an end. I didn't let myself think about the kind of life he must be living. But lately . . ."

"It's hard to stay objective," Liz agreed. "I once spent a week working at a halfway house. We tried to get kids in off the streets, if only for a cup of hot chocolate and one night's sleep in a bed. I couldn't do it. You have to wall off too much of yourself; you can't let yourself see them as what they really are or you'll burn out."

He made no immediate reply to that, and she was lost for a moment thinking about that time; though it had been only a week, it seemed there were enough memories from it to fill a year. She recalled most vividly the desperate pride of those lost children in who they were and what they did, the rationalizations that let them preserve self-respect while on the stroll or shooting up. She remembered passing out condoms and bleach to thirteen-year-olds, watching paramedics giving CPR to a girl who had gone into fibrillation with the needle still between her toes, seeing the heart-and-trident tattoo that identified an appointed gang executioner on the arm of a boy not even old enough to shave.

"They make it real simple in books and on TV," she said softly. "All those young blond goddesses plucked from the hearths of Middle America by evil black pimps, winding up walking Broadway in hot pants and halter tops. It isn't like that. It's the families more than the pimps who are responsible. The kids run to the streets because the streets are better than their homes. It's that simple." She looked at Scott. "You say Thayer wants his son back. I have to wonder if he deserves to have him back."

"That's not my business," Scott said. "I was hired to find the boy, not make judgments about his family. After all, we don't know for sure what drove him to the streets."

Liz sighed, suddenly feeling very tired. "I suppose you're right." She stepped up to him and kissed him lightly on the mouth, noticing his eyes widen in surprise. "Thanks for a pleasant evening."

He smiled, and for the first time his face seemed to lose, for a moment, its guarded expression. "Thanks for introducing me to sushi. I like California rolls."

"Next time we'll try you on sashimi. 'Night." Liz entered the building, pausing after the first few steps up the stairs and looking back. She could only see his feet from this angle. He stood there for a moment before walking off.

Well, she thought. The detective turned out not to be a dickweed after all. In fact, if the truth be known, he seemed a pretty nice guy. Just how nice, and how nice she was prepared to be in return, was still by no means certain. But the memory of a pleasant evening was enough to take with her up the cold silent stairs to her empty apartment.

RUSSELL STOOD ON THE deck of the ferry, looking back at the wall of fog that shrouded San Francisco, and from which the boat had just emerged. It was like coming out of some other dimension back to reality. The thought made him smile wanly; Danny Thayer would probably look at it that way.

But for the first time in the past few days, he did not want to think about the missing boy. His mind was instead full of remembered images of Liz Gallegher. It seemed hard to believe that when he had first met her he had not liked her at all. That had definitely changed, though

138

Russell was not sure how far past "like" he was willing to go in describing his feelings for her. But the nicest part of it all, surprisingly enough, was that he felt no anxiety about where it would go from here. In the past, whenever the possibility of a relationship had reared its ugly head, he had always felt a consuming need to know exactly where they were with each other. Would they sleep together? If so, when? And if not, why not? Were they in love? Would they be sharing an apartment anytime in the near future? And whose—his or hers?

And so on. More than once Russell's need to have questions like this answered, or at least discussed, in the early stages had nipped budding romance long before it had a chance to flower. He could not understand it; he had always seemed content enough to let his life meander along from day to day, without much thought for the future. But whenever he met a woman who showed the slightest bit of interest in him, he became a control freak.

Russell shrugged, feeling oddly at peace with himself. A strange feeling; he knew that if he pushed at and questioned it long enough it would dissolve, and he did not particularly want it to. It was enough to know that he did not feel any need to have those questions answered this time. The sense of serenity was puzzling, but pleasing. He was content, for the first time that he could remember, simply to let his connection with Liz be whatever it was. Should it evolve into something else, well and good. If not, then that was as it should be.

He had sought this feeling of clarity and peacefulness all his life, it suddenly seemed. He remembered vividly, though it was more than twenty years ago, his only acid trip. He had been talked into trying the chemical by some friends. It had not been a pleasant experience. The hallucinations had been disappointing to him; he remem-

139

bered being surprised at how similar they were to cinematic depictions of psychedelic effects. The powerful taste of it had seemed to suffuse every cell of him, and the loss of control over his senses and his body—he recalled trying to eat a banana and not being able to find his mouth—had been frightening. There were those who said LSD showed the way to enlightenment, but not as far as Scott Russell had been concerned. He hadn't even been able to find the way to the bathroom while on it.

He watched the lights of Sausalito approaching. Soon he would be back aboard his tiny houseboat, alone with the meager accumulations of his life so far. And yet the thought did not depress him. He remembered reading once that there are as many definitions of success as there are people to define it. For the first time in memory, he did not feel like a failure. Perhaps it was only the cold wind off the bay, but as the ferry pulled into the dock Scott Russell realized he had tears in his eyes.

13

Danny, Robin and her friends were still in the Haight district the following morning. They had slept most comfortably in a bed-and-breakfast establishment; the owner had taken no notice of them entering.

Despite the comfortable bed, Danny had had a hard time getting to sleep. He tossed and turned, thinking of his failure to impress Robin and the other scatterlings in the underground chamber beneath the cable museum. Patch had made no effort to hide his contempt, and even Robin had seemed disappointed.

Robin believed he had magic in him, as did he—but how to *reach* it? He had never seen the slightest bit of evidence of it, after all. What if it were buried too deeply within him for him to reach?

What if it did not exist within him at all?

THE FOLLOWING MORNING, AFTER they had left the hostel and were wandering aimlessly up Haight, Robin looked at him and said, "It's time we taught you some things, Danny."

The day was gray and overcast, with drifts of fog eddying in the gutters and at the bottom of hills. It looked to Danny like some strange netherland where different times and different worlds intersected. Here it was still the colorful Sixties haven that it had been for so many years, despite the encroachments of yuppiedom. It seemed every block had a food co-op or a head shop.

They stopped in front of the Anarchist Collective Bookstore. Danny could hear Jimi Hendrix's tortured guitar blasting from a stereo system in an upstairs apartment nearby. "We gonna do some spare-changin'?" he asked.

The others did not answer. Robin crouched on the sidewalk a little bit away from them. It was early, and there were few people on the street. Those who did pass them paid little attention to Robin. Danny thought for a moment that he saw a shimmering sort of light playing about her hands, which were cupped a few inches above a crack in the sidewalk, but it might just have been the early morning sun reflecting from a nearby wine bottle.

Then she moved, and he saw to his surprise that a flower had sprouted from the crack in the sidewalk. He could have sworn that it had not been there a moment ago. A single blossom, looking somewhat like a lily but with petals a shade somewhere between rose and gold, lifted delicately toward the sky. Robin pinched the flower from its stem, and Danny's jaw dropped as he saw the leafy stalk wither away in an instant to a dry twig.

Robin came toward him, holding the flower. "Sniff it," she said.

Danny did as she bid. The flower's scent was delicate and at the same time very strong, clearing his head almost

142

as a nasal inhalant would. Some sort of drug? he won-dered. But that seemed silly—why would scatterlings need drugs of any sort when they had magic?

Then he looked about him, and knew that if it was a drug, it was one unlike any that he had ever experienced before.

The street and the people and cars on it did not seem to have changed, in one sense. There were no enhanced colors, no melting structures like he had experienced on acid. And yet, in another, subtler sense, everything had changed. Danny realized that he was seeing the street, the people—everything—*exactly as it was*. There was no other way to put it. He knew that he was looking at reality, unadorned by preconceptions and emotions, for the first time in his life.

He took a deep breath, feeling the air reaching far into his lungs. He looked at his hands, then turned and examined himself in the reflection of the store window. It was him, Danny Thayer—purely and simply him. He did not feel particularly powerful or strong, as he had the one time he had done coke. But he knew that the image before him was exact and true, and he felt connected with every cell of it.

Danny became gradually aware that Robin was speak-ing. "The Folk have a magic called glamour—it can hide things, change appearances, fool most people when nec-essary. Humans have a kind of glamour as well, only they don't know it. It hides the true nature of things—and of themselves—from them. They see the world as they want to see it, or as others teach them to see it. Though you're one of us, you still see things as you've been taught by all the humans around you. It's time you got to know your-self."

"What do you want me to do?" Danny found he had no

trouble understanding what she was saying, though it did not seem that she was speaking English.

Puck turned to a nearby wall and put his finger to it. He moved it across the rough surface, and Danny saw letters appear, seemingly scorched into the wall by Puck's finger, a magical tagging that required no can of spray-paint. A few moments ago this would have astounded him. Now he knew it was simply what it was, and as such was no cause for excitement.

"Can you read this?" he asked after he had finished.

At first he did not think he could, because what Puck had written was by no means English, and Danny could not read even English all that well. But then it occurred to him that all languages were really the same, just marks made on a surface, and that there was no reason for him not to be able to read it.

"It says 'The City Under the Hill,'" he said. He did not feel particularly proud of himself. It was just something he could do.

The scatterlings looked at each other. Normally Danny had trouble reading the emotions that passed between them, but not so now. They were pleased. He wondered fleetingly why they should be.

Robin stepped up to him, looking into his eyes. "Can you feel it now?" she asked. "Can you feel the power inside you? Reach for it, Danny. *Feel* it."

He tried. He closed his eyes and concentrated, trying to go inside himself, to the part that was just as real as all the rest of him, just as real as all the world outside him. It was there; he could sense it. But something locked it away from him.

"You *have* reached it before," Robin was saying from far away. "You used it the night you met me, to see

144

through the glamour and find me. Find it again, Danny. Find it again!"

It was no use. There were things he could do, and things he could not do. This was one of the latter. Danny opened his eyes and saw them react in disappointment. He felt a faint echo of it within himself. He looked around—the world looked subtly different somehow, not quite as *real*. Danny realized that the effect of the flower was wearing off.

He also knew that when it did, he was going to be very unhappy with himself again.

JAKE AND SEVERAL MEMBERS of the Aryan Apostles were on the hunt. He had a gut certainty that his quarry were to be found somewhere in the Haight. And if they did not come upon the same bunch of assholes they had tried to trash the day before, no big deal—there were plenty of other targets.

Then he saw them. They were coming out of a comic-book store a block ahead of them. Spike and Thomas saw them at the same time, and cast nervous glances at Jake. The latter slipped one hand into his pocket, feeling the oiled metal of the gun there, and smiled. "Let's go," he said.

THE SCATTERLINGS LED DANNY down a side street and into a fire-gutted old Victorian awaiting restoration. It had once been painted in Day-Glo colors, and a big marijuana plant was still etched in stained glass above the front door. In a blackened upstairs room the scatterlings sat on the floor around Danny, making him feel uncomfortably like he was on trial.

Patch said, "It's just not going to work, Robin. Nothing's getting through to him."

145

Danny could see the disappointment in Robin's face, could hear it in her voice as she said, "I admit I'm running out of ideas." More than anything else in the world, he did not want to let her down.

"I'm trying, Robin," he said, the note of desperate pleading in his voice making them all look at him. He had always been a disappointment to everyone in his life. Something told him these scatterlings were his last hope of a family, and the thought of letting Robin down filled him with despair. But he did not know what to do to make things any better. He felt the desire to cry rising up in his throat, and although he did not want to show weakness in front of them, especially Patch, he knew it was futile to try to stop the tears.

It was then that the skinheads burst into the room.

WHEN DANNY SAW THE three leap into the room, guns in their hands, he did the only thing he could think of to do: he pulled the raygun from the waistband of his jeans and pointed it at the one with the swastika on his scalp, who was closest to Danny. The toy looked enough like a real gun in the dim light of the hall to cause Spike to step backward hastily, forgetting for the moment the gun he held. He stepped on an empty beer bottle lying on the floor, which rolled beneath him, causing him to lose his balance. He fell heavily, cracking his head on the floor, and lay still.

Jake—Danny recognized him from the park yesterday—pointed a gun at him. "Eat this, asshole!" he shouted.

Time slowed to a crawl for Danny. He could clearly see the finger tightening on the trigger. Now was the time, he knew, to call upon the power within him, if it was in fact there.

But he could not. His mind fluttered frantically, like a

panicked bird in a cage. And in the instant Jake pulled the trigger, at the same time Robin hurled herself in front of Danny.

The bullet struck her in the chest, hurling her back against him. They both fell to the floor, Robin on top of him. He screamed something wordless and despairing, realizing that she had given her life to protect him. To save someone not worth saving.

There were shouts and sounds of struggling as the other scatterlings closed in on Jake and his cohort. He heard a gun go off again, though he had no idea who, if anyone, had been shot. And then he felt again the subtle soundless cracking of power in the room. At the same time he realized that Robin no longer sprawled across him. He rolled over and looked up to see Robin standing over him, feet braced and arms upraised. And he also saw the most amazing thing—the two skinheads, with their tattoos of dripping knives and Nazi symbols, were cowering back as though they faced the Frankenstein monster.

Robin grabbed Danny and pulled him to his feet. "Come on!" she shouted. "The illusion won't last long!" They turned and ran toward the upstairs window, along with the others. "Jump!" she hissed in his ear.

"Are you crazy?"

"No; just desperate. Now *jump!*"

Danny gulped, closed his eyes, and jumped.

He had fallen once from a fairly great height as a boy; over twenty feet off the roof of the family home. What he remembered most about it was the momentary sensation of floating, the eerie feeling of all his internal organs in freefall within him, and, even more vividly, the building rush of air past his ears. It was that growing shriek of air that had frightened him the most, for it told him in graphic terms of the increasing speed of his fall.

Now he felt the first sensation, that of weightlessness, but there was no howling wind against his face. Danny's eyes snapped open and he bit down hard to choke back a cry.

They were *floating* down the side of the building!

There was little time to be amazed, much less to enjoy the experience. By the time Danny realized what was going on, the controlled fall was over, and Robin was running, pulling him along, with the rest of the scatterlings behind them. They hurried down several side streets before they finally stopped.

Danny was breathing in hard, ragged gasps. With an effort, he managed to control it. One small part of his mind realized that his raygun was gone; probably it had fallen from his hand when they were descending from the window.

Robin was leaning against a tree, eyes closed. He stared at her, realizing that there was no sign of blood or a wound—though he had seen her shot point-blank. "What—what happened?" Danny finally managed to ask Puck.

"Robin gave them what used to be known as an elf-shot," the small scatterling replied. "When they recover, they won't remember anything of it."

"I didn't mean that. I saw her get shot—"

Robin opened her eyes. "Only iron can kill us, Danny. That bullet was made of lead."

Patch said, "He couldn't use his power even when his life depended on it. Face it, Robin—there's no way to reach him."

Robin looked at Danny. Though he felt ashamed, he forced himself to meet her gaze—and saw in it a great pity, and a great sadness. "What do we do now?" he asked quietly.

She sighed. "I think," she said, "that it's time for desperate measures."

PART TWO

THE LOOKING GLASS

No matter how fair the sun shines, still must it set.
—*The Maiden from Fairyland*
Ferdinand Raimund

Which of us is not forever a stranger and alone?
—*Look Homeward, Angel*
Thomas Wolfe

14

Edward Thayer contemplated the view from his office suite window. Six stories below him was Ventura Boulevard, lined with office buildings, expensive restaurants and trendy shops. Beyond several blocks of houses could be seen the Ventura Freeway, its traffic crawling sluggishly along as usual, even though it was only the middle of the afternoon. Thayer wondered idly why there were so many cars on the freeways and streets of Los Angeles at all hours. Were so many people out of work, or possessed of the kinds of jobs that allowed them to flit about in the middle of the day?

Of course this wasn't Los Angeles, strictly speaking. This was Encino, in the San Fernando Valley. Thayer's eyebrows drew together ever so slightly. It was not where he had hoped to be at the age of forty-six . . . still, all things considered, he had not done poorly. True, a business address in Century City, with its coveted nine-double-zero zip, was far more prestigious. Still, if one had to work in the coventry of the 818 area code, Encino was not a bad place to be. And his building was on the south side of the Boulevard.

"Mr. Thayer?" The words came softly from the intercom on the desk behind him. He did not turn around. "Yes?"

"Daniel Presky from Touchstone is on line three."

"Not now," Thayer said.

A moment's uncertainty seemed to hang in the still, filtered air before his secretary said, "Yes sir. I'll tell him you'll call him back."

"No. Just tell him Chasen's at one tomorrow. One exactly."

"Yes sir."

Thayer continued to gaze out his window. He could see his ghostly reflection in the tinted floor-to-ceiling glass, superimposed like a giant astride the Boulevard, towering against the iron-gray sky. A somewhat overweight giant, it was true, but still tanned and in quite good physical shape for his age—his thrice-weekly workouts with his private trainer accounted for that. The haircut, the tie—puce, the current power color—and the suit, not to mention the steel and mahogany furnishings behind him, all attested to his success in a very mercurial and cutthroat industry. He had come a long way from the lower-middle-class Kansas City home where he had grown up. His company, Wheatfield Productions, was responsible for six films, the latest of which had grossed a respectable eighty million so far in domestic release. He owned a house just off Mulholland Drive and several apartment buildings in Boyle Heights, which he rented to quite a few families of illegal aliens. He was, by any definition anyone would care to apply, a success.

Still, there had been . . . failures.

He turned toward his desk. On the rich black surface,

next to a stack of scripts that bore unctuous notes from agents, was a picture of his wife. She was smiling, though the eyes showed a certain amount of strain. Perhaps six inches from that frame was another, smaller one, containing a photograph of his son. Danny's smile was no more sincere than Estelle's. Thayer stared at the photo without expression for a moment before he spoke.

"Jenny, get me Scott Russell in Sausalito again."

His secretary acknowledged the order in a quiet voice. Thayer sat down, scowling at his hands where they rested on the desktop.

Danny. He thought of a small child, barely able to walk, hanging on to his fingers and laughing, or waddling awkwardly toward him, arms outstretched for a hug. Whenever he thought of his son it was always as a baby or a toddler—his mind hesitated to encompass pictures of the boy beyond the age of three. And the last six or seven years seemed memories of nothing but grief. But those first few years had held hope, both for his marriage and his son . . .

"Mr. Thayer? There's no answer."

"Thank you." He could feel anger beginning to build inside him now. He welcomed it; it was much more satisfying to feel something—anything—than the stony coldness that filled him these days when he looked at Danny's picture. It was better than hearing the small voice that whispered to him in the furthest part of his mind that he was better off as long as Danny was missing, or perhaps even . . .

He shook his head once, sharply. No. He *would* find the boy. Russell was his last chance—he would see some results out of hiring him or know the reason why. And if he could not contact him by phone, well—there were other ways.

153

He spoke to the intercom again. "Book me a flight into San Francisco. Tonight."

ALICE WAS PARTICULARLY ENJOYING herself this day. It was just foggy and cold enough outside to make her glad to be inside, where she could stand under the ceiling vents and feel the warm air blowing on her face or prowl down well-known narrow aisles to straighten and realphabetize titles.

The only fly in the ointment was that Mao had still not returned. The cat had been missing for three days now, and Alice was beginning to think that he would not be back. She had felt very alone in her little apartment above the store these past few nights.

The bells at the door announced the arrival of another customer. She glanced toward the front of the shop and saw a tall old man enter. He was wearing a sweater and slacks, and had a magnificent mane of thick white hair. His face looked vaguely familiar to her. Frowning, she tried to place it . . .

By the time she did, he had found the mythology section and was selecting books from the shelves. She hurried up to him. "Mr. Craig, isn't it? Douglas Francis Craig?"

The man nodded. He looked somewhat bemused, as if he was being dragged back reluctantly from the private world of his thoughts.

"I'm Alice Kopfman, the owner. I just wanted to tell you how much I've enjoyed your work."

Craig peered at her rather distractedly from beneath bushy white eyebrows. Alice was impressed by how tall he was; of course, she reminded herself, when one is only five foot five almost everyone over fifteen years old is tall. Still, Craig had an impressive air to him, which was augmented

154

by his silken white hair and not particularly mitigated by his somewhat shabby clothes.

She realized that he was looking at her as an absent-minded instructor might gaze at a particularly precocious student. After a moment, however, he smiled. "Thank you," he said. His voice was just what she expected it would be: rich, almost oratorical. He must have been quite striking twenty years ago, she thought. He's not bad now.

"You have a lovely store here, quite well stocked," he continued, glancing about. Alice felt a moment of panic at not having a ready reply. She heard herself saying, "I assume you've looked at the photography row in our art section."

He smiled again. It was a very gentle smile, with no hint of hidden amusement; she liked that. "Not yet. I'm always afraid of being disappointed."

"I think you'll find yourself well represented. We have several of your earlier collections, including *British Dawn,* which is hard to get in this country."

He looked slightly surprised and impressed at that, and Alice felt absurdly pleased with herself. "I *am* impressed—that was quite a limited run."

"I have a very good British distributor." She glanced down at the stack of books by his feet. Froud and Lee's art book, Brigg's *Encyclopedia of Fairies*, *The Lavender Fairy Book* . . . "You seem quite interested in fairies, Mr. Craig."

"Doug, please."

Alice smiled. There was a definite rapport here; she could feel it, and she was fairly sure that he could feel it too. She had gone out with men since Clark's death, of course—had even had a few affairs, one of which lasted over a year. But there had been no one serious in her life

155

for some time now, and, looking at Doug Craig, she suddenly knew that she was ready for that to change.

"There's a fantasy novel that's all about fairies: *The City Under the Hill*, by Donald McTosh. We sell a fair number of copies. It's downstairs in our fantasy section." She started toward the stairs, beckoning to him to follow, which he did. As she passed beneath one of the convex mirrors placed to spot shoplifters, she glanced up at herself quickly, trying to note the condition of her blusher and whether the imperfect heating of the old store had caused her mascara to form raccoon eyes. Everything seemed in order. Alice smiled at herself. She had not played this game in some time; it was gratifying to realize that it was just as much fun this late in her life as it had ever been.

DOUGLAS CRAIG WAS ENJOYING the game just as much, somewhat to his surprise. Alice Kopfman had picked precisely the right moment to approach him. He had spent the past day and a half visiting several bookstores in the area and amassing a collection of books on fairies, elves, sprites and other kindred subjects, and he was beginning to feel quite overwhelmed. What he needed was someone to take him by the hand and lead him for a time in his quest. Which was precisely what Alice appeared to be doing.

On top of that he found her honestly attractive, in a much more substantial manner than the momentary wistful lust he experienced now and again when passing women on the street. He had been largely celibate since his divorce—liquor had been his mistress, and a very possessive one.

She had possessed him again, despite his resolution to the contrary; when the shakes and headaches of alcohol withdrawal had begun he had given in and dulled the pain.

156

However, he had not kept drinking. That was something, at least.

At this moment he was caught between considering Alice Kopfman a welcome diversion for conversation, someone to take his mind off this increasingly unbelievable search he had begun, or someone whose brain he might pick for still more information about fairies. He was not sure which course to pursue. He had little doubt that, should he slacken in his single-minded pursuit of his quarry, he would soon find himself looking at the world through the bottom of a glass again. Craig did not particularly fear that fate—it had held no terrors for him for many years—but he was concerned that he would lose the trail, if there indeed was one.

On the other hand, here was a woman he liked, who obviously liked him. He decided to see where the moment went after she found him the novel.

Downstairs, Craig watched her move along the aisles, running a practiced finger down the spines of the books and clucking her tongue now and again as she found a volume out of place. "Here it is." She pulled a paperback from the shelf and handed it to him. He glanced at it, noticing a pastoral scene of castles and fey characters on the cover before he returned his gaze to hers. He knew then that he was going to ask her to dinner, and it was a very comfortable and warm thing to know.

He heard a faint tinkling of bells from upstairs and saw a distracted look enter her eyes for a moment. He realized that a customer had entered; she had her job to do, but she also did not want to spoil this moment. Quickly, then:

"Would you have dinner with me tonight, Alice Kopfman?"

157

"I would be delighted, Douglas Craig."

As easy as that.

ONCE AGAIN EDWARD THAYER stood before a window looking down at the city below. This time, however, he was in a suite at the Hyatt in downtown San Francisco, gazing at the crowds of people moving through the maze of box hedges in Union Square. It was morning, and the fog that had wreathed the city for several hours had lifted at least temporarily.

He had just tried to call Scott Russell again and again gotten no answer. He hoped that this prolonged absence meant the man was hot on the trail of his missing son.

He turned away from the window to the bar and poured himself a drink. He had come up here on what could only be described as impulse, canceling several important meetings in the process. He could not really say why he had come, and that frightened him. He did not think of himself as a man given to impulsive behavior. Yet here he was.

He glanced at the phone. The operator had told him that the prefix of Russell's number placed it in Sausalito, but she had not been able to find an address to go with it. Of course, Thayer thought with a slight twitch of his lips, he could always hire a detective to find the detective he had hired to find Danny. He looked at the hand holding the glass and noticed it was shaking ever so slightly. He frowned. Russell would have to return sooner or later.

No one knew he had come here, not even his wife. He had told her he had to fly to New York for an emergency budget meeting. She had not protested; years before, she had stopped objecting to anything he did. He doubted if she would have even noticed his absence had he not told her; the loss of her son had driven her even further into the bottle. Thayer sat the drink down abruptly. To succumb to alcohol—or any sort of drug—was weak. He was not weak. He had never fallen prey to liquor, cocaine or any other temptations of that sort. If he had an addiction, it was power.

He wanted Danny back.

He picked up the phone again. His finger did not tremble as he pressed the numbers.

"WELL," SCOTT SAID, "THIS was an unexpected pleasure."

Beside him Liz Gallegher stretched languidly, her naked form half-concealed by the bed's heavy comforter. "Yeah, well, I kinda enjoyed it too, believe it or not."

Scott looked with interest around the bedroom. It was even messier, if possible, than his place, with clothes hanging over chairs, on closet doors, and piled in various untidy heaps. At least a week's worth of newspapers was scattered on the floor, and a desk in the far corner was nearly buried beneath magazines and typewritten sheets of paper. On a wall shelf directly across from him was an impressive collection of spring-driven toys, the kind that, when wound up, would stroll about aimlessly or do backflips. Scott could see, among others, a pair of teeth, several dinosaurs, plastic replicas of different types of sushi, and a miniature Godzilla.

He grinned at Liz. "Last night you didn't even invite me up. I sure as hell didn't expect to spend the night after our second date."

"Maybe it was the wine we had after dinner. Or maybe it was just you saying that you wanted to sleep with me. Men should try that more often with women. They'd be surprised."

"After last night, nothing can surprise me."

Liz kissed him, then got out of bed. Scott watched her

159

pull a housecoat from the closet and put it on, more in reaction to the morning chill than out of modesty. Her body was lithe and tight—he'd been surprised by how muscular she was. "Sorry about insisting on the condom, by the way," she said.

"No problem. You can't be too careful. Though it is like taking a shower with a wetsuit on."

She laughed. "Get up. I'm going to get dressed and make coffee, and then I've got to get to the office."

COFFEE WAS ANOTHER SURPRISE: Jamaica Blue Mountain, freshly ground. It seemed rather out of place to be drinking expensive gourmet coffee in Liz's tiny kitchen, with its sink full of dirty dishes and a redolent cat box next to the refrigerator.

"I didn't know you had a cat."

"Cats. Two. They don't suffer strangers gladly."

Scott cupped his chin in his palm and leaned his elbow on the table. He smiled at Liz and exhaled a deep, satisfied sigh.

She looked wary. "Don't."

"Don't what?"

"Don't fall in love, okay? Not yet, anyway. Let's have a sense of perspective about this."

He spread his hands in a gesture of puzzlement. "What can I say? I'm a sensitive kinda guy. When I spend a night having fantastic sex with an attractive woman, I feel a certain residual affection the next day. Call me a sentimental fool."

Liz looked at him for a moment as though deciding whether or not to be annoyed, then smiled slightly. "That was a truly impressive display of sarcasm, shamus. I didn't know you had it in you."

"It comes and goes. And please don't call me 'sha-

160

mus.' Or 'gumshoe.' Or 'peeper.' And *especially* not 'dick.' "

"I'm sorry. I just wanted to be sure that you knew that, while I don't sleep with everyone who knocks on my office door, I don't have to be committed to a lifelong relationship with somebody either."

Scott was beginning to feel slightly annoyed. "Don't worry. I'm not planning on subletting my houseboat and moving in."

"I know, I was just— You have a houseboat?"

He laughed. After a moment she joined in. The laughter was honest and pure, a moment of companionship as close in its own way as what they had shared last night. "Yeah, over in Sausalito. I call it a houseboat because 'floating corrugated tin shack' is too big a mouthful. It would probably be considered pretty snazzy by some Third World standards." He looked at her expression. "You're surprised."

"Well, yeah. You don't look nearly that . . . bohemian."

Scott tried to look wise and mysterious. It evidently was not a complete success, because Liz began to laugh again. "What's funny now?"

"I just realized," she sputtered, "that I spent the night with Travis McGee!"

"Who's Travis McGee?" The question caused her to laugh so hard that she had to set her coffee cup down to avoid spilling it.

"I'm sorry." She wiped her eyes with her napkin. "Jesus, there's got to be a story in this . . . no, don't get upset," she added hastily. "I just mean—you're just who you are, aren't you? You're just this guy who's a detective—"

"*Was* a detective—"

"—who lives on a houseboat and is trying to find this missing kid, and you're just—you're just *that.*"

161

Scott could not determine if Liz was making fun of him or not. "Yeah, I guess I am," he didn't quite snap. "So what?"

She looked at him for a long moment, then took his hand in hers and said, very seriously, "So I think that's great."

15

The next morning—gray, misty and cold—found Danny and the scatterlings back at his old haunts of Broadway near Chinatown. They had spent the night sleeping in a twenty-four-hour porn theater, despite Danny's urging that the scatterlings use their magic to procure more congenial lodgings. His new friends seemed occasionally to enjoy the grittiness of street life, a point of view Danny found as baffling as he did frustrating.

He treated them to breakfast by phoning a Pizza Hut and ordering two large pizzas, then waiting in the alley near the dumpster until they threw out the unclaimed food. After that they wandered aimlessly up and down Broadway for a time. This was singularly useless in Danny's opinion, as the strip of nightclubs and restaurants was only good pickings at night.

He could not get Robin to tell him what she had meant by her cryptic statement that it was time for "desperate measures." He did not press her too much, however; although he was scared of the power that they believed dwelled within him, he was also in love with Robin, and trusted her.

Despite his feelings for her, however, Danny was on the whole profoundly depressed. It seemed to him that he was blowing his chances of ever going to Fairyland, and the thought filled him with conflicting fear and relief. The idea of leaving this world for a new one was frightening in the extreme; however, to stay here was to continue in a hopeless, brutal existence, with no chance of ever rising above it.

He could not help thinking about his family; specifically, about his father. When these reminiscences overwhelmed him, his mother occupied very little memory space. If he had any emotions toward her at all, they were mostly anger and contempt at the way she pretended that nothing was happening, that they were really a happy, loving, "Cosby Show" family. Still, in a way he could understand her not being able to stand up to Edward Thayer. His father had been so overwhelming, so all-powerful in his decrees and desires, that no one—save, perhaps, the champions and superheroes with which Danny populated his fantasy world—could possibly resist him.

Certainly he had not been able to . . .

He became aware that Robin was looking searchingly at him as they walked along the sidewalk. "You're thinking about your father," she said.

He did not ask how she knew, or try to deny it—instead he mumbled an assent. "Tell me about him," Robin said gently. "What's his name? What does he do?"

He told her. "He's a producer—you know, movies. Pretty famous. He knows a lot of movie stars." He could not help feeling a small glimmer of pride as he said this.

"You don't love him." It was not a question.

He laughed—a short, sharp, bitter sound that drew glances from passersby. "No kidding. I wish he was dead."

He expected her to ask more questions about why he hated his father with such intensity, and was somewhat surprised when she did not. It was, perhaps, her silence that caused him to volunteer more information. "He . . . did things to me," he said, unable to speak in more than a mumble. It was more than he had ever told anyone else, even Roberto. He huddled deeper into his denim jacket.

"I understand," Robin replied. Merely two words, spoken so softly as to barely be heard, and yet Danny felt his heart nearly burst within him in reaction. At that moment he would gladly have died to have brought even a momentary smile to her face.

As they proceeded down the street he saw someone he recognized approaching: an old panhandler who called himself the Sorcerer. Though he talked a lot about black magic and had a third eye tattooed on his forehead, Danny knew that the Sorcerer was not really a wizard, merely an aging Sixties relic who had taken one too many acid trips.

He saw Danny and his craggy face creased into a smile of recognition. "Hey, wow, man, how's it goin'? Haven't seen you on the street lately."

"Been workin' North Beach," Danny told him. "How's the con around here nowadays?"

"Not too great. Off season for tourists. 'Ja hear about Shanti?"

Danny felt the chill air suddenly stab deep within him. "What happened?"

"Bummer, man. She rode the Nimitz with some devo suit. Cops had a hard time I.D.-ing her, she was so cut up."

They exchanged a few more words, the gist of which Danny would not remember later. The Sorcerer then

165

moved on down Broadway, his tattered nylon windbreaker flapping in the cold breeze.

Danny sagged against a graffiti-marred wall as Robin and the other scatterlings looked curiously at him. When she asked him what was wrong, all he could say was, "It didn't work."

"What didn't work?"

"The spellstone. I gave it to her to protect her, and it didn't."

He saw them exchange baffled glances, but he could say nothing further to enlighten them. His mind was full of thoughts of Shanti. They had not been that close—they had only slept together a few times, as much for comfort and warmth as for sex—but she had been part of the tenuous network that was all he had in the way of a family. And in addition to the sorrow Danny felt at her passing, there was the graphic evidence that his magic had not worked for her—and if it had not worked for Shanti, how could he expect it to do what the scatterlings wanted?

How could he hope that it would take him home?

DOUGLAS FRANCIS CRAIG WAS feeling quite happy as he arrived back at his Pacific Heights townhouse that evening. His dinner with Alice had been a very enjoyable experience. They had dined at a seafood grill in Fort Mason, and then strolled along the Marina Green, enjoying the sunset. Alice had shown a considerable knowledge of photography, not only of his work but of other artists as well. She was very well read, and they found that they shared likes and dislikes of quite a few authors and films—and on the ones on which they disagreed, they did so agreeably. All in all, Craig told himself as he entered the code to disarm the house alarm and unlocked the door, it was one of the most pleasant outings he had had in quite

166

some time. And one of the best parts about it was that he had made his drink of choice during the dinner club soda.

He paused a moment in the foyer, as was his habit, to enjoy returning home. This townhouse had been his sanctum for many years, and he was quite proud of it. It had been one of the lucky ones in the Loma Pieta quake—there had been only minor structural damage, easily repaired. He hung up his coat, pausing momentarily to admire a framed early Steichen as he entered the living room. He might be a drunkard, Craig told himself complacently, but he was not a sloppy one—his house was always neat and clean. The glass and chrome decor might be a bit passé, but it suited him. And although three stories were almost embarrassingly large for a single man to call home in crowded San Francisco, still he had no desire to sell it, even though the stairs were getting harder and harder to climb.

He avoided the downstairs den with the bar, going instead into the living room. With a groan of relief he dropped the large bag of books he had bought from Alice's bookshop and began to sort through them, stacking them in neat piles on the cocktail table. Alice had been quite interested in his fascination with fairies, but he had not told her the reasons behind it. He did not trust her that much yet—perhaps he never would. Also, he certainly did not want to scare her away, and he was sure that telling her that he was looking for an entrance into Faerie would accomplish that quite nicely.

Whether it was a mad quest or not, however, at least it was giving his life some meaning and keeping him out of the bottle. If that constituted insanity, then Craig was all for it. He looked at the last book to come out of the bag—the fantasy novel called *The City Under the Hill*. Though he had intended to start his research with one of the nonfiction books, he decided instead—he was not sure why—to glance through the first chapter of this instead. He settled down in a comfortable leather chair, adjusted the reading lamp just so, and opened the paperback. All that was missing was a drink at his elbow. Craig turned quickly to the first page and started to read.

HE WAS A BIT startled when he looked up at the clock and saw that it was nearly three A.M.; he had been reading for almost five hours. He was hard-pressed to say what it was about the book that fascinated him so, save that it dealt with a nostalgia and yearning for things that might have been. And a vague unease as well; he could not shake the feeling that there was more truth than fiction in the book's contention that Faerie and Earth were slowly and irrevocably drawing apart. The thought filled Craig with sadness; if it were true, then his chance to return to Faerie might already be lost.

He stood, stretched, feeling bones and ligaments creak, and crossed to the glass door that looked out on the terrace. From here he could see the lights of the Golden Gate, as well as Richmond and the Presidio. Though it was late at night, there were still some cars on the streets, and even people, though not many.

Oddly enough, he felt no desire for a drink, although the night was usually his time of greatest temptation. He thought of Alice, no doubt snugly asleep in her apartment above her picturesque store, and felt a stirring of desire for her that was as much loneliness as ardor. He had been quite content living by himself for many years, but now the townhouse suddenly seemed entirely too big and coldly impersonal for him.

What if his research were to pay off—what if, against all rationality, he discovered a way to leave this world for

Faerie again? Would he want to leave what might well be a new romance for him, the first one in years?

Craig told himself not to get carried away. There were all kinds of possibilities extant, after all, not the least of which was that neither his search nor his attraction to Alice would pan out. It made no sense to worry about it, certainly not now, when he ought to be sound asleep.

He turned out the lights and climbed the stairs to the bedroom. He slept on a waterbed; he found it much easier on his back than a regular mattress. Usually he had no trouble dropping off to sleep, but tonight he was still awake even after the first faint ribbons of dawn began to color the eastern sky.

DANNY RELAXED BETWEEN CLEAN sheets, luxuriating in the rare comfort of a firm mattress in a warm, clean room. His importunings for decent lodgings had finally had an effect, and the scatterlings had used their magic to procure rooms at a hotel downtown. After spending some time in the lobby admiring the murals, suits of armor and vaulted gold-leaf ceiling, they had retired to their two-room suite. Danny had dined sumptuously from the room service menu, and was now well on his way to dreamland.

He was not quite asleep, however; the connecting door was open, and he could hear Robin and Patch deep in conversation. He drifted comfortably in that limbo state between sleep and wakefulness, hearing their dialogue without really processing it.

Patch said, "Suppose we don't die. It's a better world here than what we had. Who says we have to die? No one knows for sure."

"Are you willing to take that chance?" Robin asked.

"It's better than going back to what I had. We all know what a scatterling's life is worth there. Here we can live as we choose. I could prowl this one city for the next five hundred years and not get tired of it."

"Well then," Robin replied, "you can stay."

"What, alone? That's no fun. C'mon, Robin—it's always been us against this world and that one. We should *all* stay." Patch added, "It's a stupid argument anyway—he can't open the gallitrap."

"I think he can. He is the Keymaster—he just can't find the lock. But he will, with the right motivation."

Patch was silent for a moment. "You really want to get back, don't you?"

"It's my home. It's *our* home. This world is exciting, entertaining—but it's not home. I don't know about you, but if I stay here forever I'll wither. I'll become nothing more than all of *them* out there—and I'd sooner die the death they die than be that."

"Okay," Patch said. "So what are you willing to do?"

Robin said, "Whatever it takes."

They were both quiet for a time, and then the conversation resumed, but by that time Danny was deeply and fully asleep.

16

"You look depressed," Liz said.

Scott was sitting in a dejected pose on the couch, desultorily playing with a wind-up toy, letting it lurch across the stained surface of the coffee table and drop to the threadbare rug. He glanced up at her words and gave her a wan smile.

She was damned if she could decide what, exactly, was attractive about him. She had never thought of herself as being particularly nurturing, and in fact felt slightly impatient, rather than supportive, with him right now. Still, the attraction was there; Liz could not deny it, and had no real inclination to.

"I'm stuck," Scott said. "Stymied. I've run out of detective stuff to throw at this problem. I've followed every lead I could dredge up on Danny Thayer, and I've got zip."

"So you're giving up?"

"No, I'm not giving up. I told you—I'm stuck. The only

thing I can do for the moment is sit here and pound my head against it until either it or my head gives."

She sat down beside him. The space heater that buzzed away nearby did little to alleviate the cold morning air, and she huddled against him as much to warm herself as to comfort him. "No more bookstore leads?"

"A clerk thinks she remembers him, but he hasn't been in there in days." Scott watched the toy—a piece of sushi with feet—stroll off the table and drop out of sight. "It's funny—when I took this job I had no intention of looking for Danny. I just figured I'd draw the check and use the time to hunt for another job. Now I'm at a point where I *have* to sit and wait for something to break—and I hate it. I feel guilty taking his father's money and not doing anything."

Liz hesitated, then said, "How about the morgue?"

"I tried that when I started. Haven't called since." He was quiet for a moment; she could not see his face. "I'd hate to find he was dead."

"You're getting too involved," Liz said. *And this conversation is beginning to sound like a TV show.* She picked up the phone. She knew the number; the morgue was one of the many regular calls she made in search of stories.

Once connected, she asked for a deputy coroner who had often given her stories on bizarre deaths in the past. Doctored up slightly, they made great copy. This time, unfortunately, he was of little help; no John Does answering Danny's description had come in recently. When she told Scott this, he merely nodded—she could not tell if he was relieved or disappointed.

Liz picked up the Yellow Pages, thumbed to the M's and tore out two pages. Then she went to the closet, took out her coat and tossed Scott his. "Come on. We have places to go."

172

He looked puzzled but put on the coat. "Places?"

"Not all bodies are taken to the morgue—the majority wind up at private mortuaries. They do the autopsies there too, if the death is suspicious. Let's check a few in the area where Danny was last seen. It beats sitting around feeling helpless."

At first she thought he was going to object, but then he shrugged and followed her out the door. Liz glanced over her shoulder at his face as they descended the stairs. It was hard and set, and she decided that further conversation might not be a good idea at the moment.

IT WAS MIDAFTERNOON WHEN they stopped at the Bayside Mortuary in the shadow of Telegraph Hill. If Scott was becoming annoyed or bored he gave no sign of it, for which Liz was profoundly grateful. They had visited seven of the somber edifices, all in the North Beach area, and she was getting ready to admit that maybe it hadn't been such a hot idea after all. Still, she could think of little else to do. If this didn't work, maybe they would have to call off the search.

She almost hoped it would be futile. She did not want to find the boy lying on a slab under fluorescent lights, but she also wanted a lead, a clue of some sort, that would give them results. She was not used to being frustrated and blocked when she wanted something, and she had to fight a growing desire to just chuck the whole thing. Which would probably not bode well for whatever tenuous thing was developing between her and Scott. She wasn't sure if that was a good idea or not.

One of the reasons she was sticking with it, she had to admit, was that part of her wanted to see Scott's face at the moment that she cracked the case, were she lucky enough to do so. Liz enjoyed competing in arenas traditionally considered male-dominated.

They spoke to the mortuary attendant—he was the seventh such professional they had encountered today, and Liz allowed herself a moment of amusement at the fact that none of them resembled the dour, saturnine movie stereotype. This one was quite young and very intense; he pondered the picture of Danny for a long time before timidly venturing an opinion.

"I don't *think* so. It's been rather a slow week, so I'm fairly sure I'd remember his face—unless, of course, it had been severely lacerated or bruised."

Liz suppressed a sigh, thanked him and held out her hand for the photo. The attendant returned it, then frowned. "What did you say his name was again?"

Scott told him. The attendant's forehead furrowed more deeply still, then smoothed abruptly. "There was a girl—just yesterday—knife wounds, I remember. Very severe. She was dead when we got her, of course, but I recall the cop who brought her in said she'd mentioned someone named 'Danny' before she died."

Liz and Scott exchanged a glance of suppressed hope. "Did she say anything else to him?" Scott asked. "Anything you can remember might be helpful to us."

"I just remember him mentioning that she had called for Danny, and then said, 'Tell him his magic didn't work.'"

"The cop who brought her in," Liz said. "We need to talk to him."

THE PHONE AWOKE DOUGLAS Craig from quite a lovely dream. In it he had followed the sprites he had seen long ago in Muir Woods through the portal and into that wondrous world that had haunted him for so many years. It had been worth the wait, Craig realized joyously; he had

174

felt the years drop away from him, had run, laughing and leaping, across star-flowered meadows, following the tinkling laughter of the fairies. No matter how fast he ran, however, he could never quite catch up with them—they remained maddeningly just beyond his reach. Their laughter had grown gradually more insistent, more strident—and had become the ringing of the phone.

Craig realized he was sitting in his favorite chair, the sleeve of his housecoat soaking in a small puddle left by his overturned drink. The fantasy novel by McTosh lay in his lap; he had fallen asleep in the warm afternoon sunlight that streamed through the window. He felt a moment of deep despairing sadness as the last vestiges of the dream dissipated, and glared at the ringing phone. How dare this person from Porlock, whoever it was, interrupt such a moment of bliss? He snatched the receiver from the cradle, then took a deep breath, reminding himself that he might be many things, but he had never been a mean drunk.

"Hello?"

The voice on the other end was female, and at first he did not recognize it. "Doug? How are you?"

"I'm fine." Then he realized who was calling him, and his momentary anger vanished as easily as had the dream. "Alice! How delightful of you to call!"

"Two things," she said. "One, I wanted to thank you for a lovely evening. Two, I wanted to let you know that we've ordered several copies of your books from Abrams, and I thought that you might be willing to autograph them. I could put up some signs in advance, and—"

"That sounds charming," Craig told her, trying to hold on to the receiver and open another bottle. "When?"

"Well, I need some time to set everything up—would Saturday be all right?"

175

"Let me check my calendar." Craig put the receiver down and steadied the bottle with one hand while opening it. He poured three fingers' worth into his glass, then picked up the receiver again. "That day seems to be free, Alice."

They exchanged a few more pleasantries before hanging up, and then he sat back in his chair with his glass. An autograph party, even an impromptu one, was a very pleasant way to spend an afternoon—and, of course, it would not hurt the sales of his books. Plus it would be made even more enjoyable by the company of Alice.

Craig glanced down at this drink, but found himself surprisingly free of guilt over having backslid yet again. He thought about the dream, but its loss did not seem so painful now either. It was much more pleasant to think about spending a Saturday afternoon with Alice in her charming bookshop, surrounded by the fruits of his labors, and perhaps even one or two people who appreciated his work. He raised the glass to his lips. Yes, there were times when life was not so bad.

"I STILL DON'T BELIEVE it," Scott said. He and Liz sat in the latter's Toyota across the street from the condemned Larkspur Hotel. The building stood out starkly against the setting sun and the skyscrapers of downtown, several blocks to the north. They were in one of the more run-down areas south of Market, full of boarded-up storefronts and graffiti-covered walls.

"No doubt about it, we got lucky," Liz agreed. The mortuary attendant had given them the name of the cop who had brought Shanti in. He had known who she was, and, more importantly, had known who Danny was and also where he usually crashed—in an abandoned hotel south of Market.

The building was surrounded by a wire fence that had been cut open in several places. A NO TRESPASSING sign hung at an odd angle. Scott considered his next move. There was no guarantee that Danny was still staying here—still, they had narrowed the search down considerably. He wondered if it would be enough for Ed Thayer.

"I could send a report to Danny's father," he mused aloud, "and let him take it from here." He grinned at Liz, feeling a warm glow within. "Son of a bitch, we did it! We solved the case!"

"Which means your meal ticket has just been punched," Liz pointed out.

Scott grimaced, remembering that he had counted on at least a week's worth of pay to see him into a new job. "Well, let's not be hasty," he said. "After all, we're still not positive that Danny lives here. Maybe a stakeout is in order."

Liz grinned. "Yeah. It might take days to establish his residence beyond doubt."

"I might even forget where the hotel is for a week or so," Scott said, grinning back. "After all, Whitaker always said I was an inept op."

They both laughed. "The sensible thing to do," Liz said, "is to go home and get some sleep. This place isn't going anywhere. You can decide what to do tomorrow, after you're rested, fed, and assured of another day's pay."

Scott nodded. "That sounds like a plan," he said as Liz cranked up the engine.

"You lookin' for somebody, man?"

The strange voice came from a man in his early twenties who was leaning on the car door on Scott's side, looking curiously through the window at them. He was tall, and despite the cold, wore a sleeveless leather vest and studded armbands. He had a faint Latin accent. But

177

what really interested Scott was the business end of the switchblade that he held within an inch of Scott's throat.

Scott glanced at Liz, who looked back at him help-lessly. The engine was running, but by the time she put it in gear and released the brake the young man with the knife could easily have carved Scott a second mouth under his chin. "Uh, yeah, I am," he said in answer to the question. "Danny Thayer. I, uh, owe him some money," he added in a burst of inspiration. He concentrated on breathing slowly and evenly. A line came to him from some old horror movie: *Don't show fear. They can sense fear.* He had to bite his tongue to keep a nervous giggle from escaping.

The knife did not waver. "Danny don't live here no more, man." Then the young man's eyes narrowed as a sudden thought occurred to him. "He'll probably come back, though. So if you owe him some money, you can just pay me. How about that, man?"

"Sounds fair." Scott hastily pulled a twenty-dollar bill from his shirt pocket—one of the ops at the agency had told him never to show his wallet in a situation like this. He handed it to the other, who stuffed it in his vest with a grin. "Tell Danny I said hello," Scott said.

"Ain't gonna tell him nothin', man. He's goin' back to Fairyland." He laughed—then, to Scott's immense relief, folded the knife and ran across the street. He ducked through one of the holes in the fence and disappeared into the unlit building.

Scott looked at Liz, and they both exhaled simulta-neous sighs of relief. Scott's heart was pounding. It was by far the most dangerous situation that his work had ever led him into.

Liz put her car in gear and accelerated quickly down

the street. "I told you I wasn't any good at this," Scott said, feeling suddenly very weak.

"You did fine." Her tone was surprisingly gentle.

"What did he mean, Danny's gone back to Fairyland? Is that street slang for some particular place?"

Liz shook her head. "Not that I know of. But it fits in—we know the kid lives in a fantasy world. The girl said before she died that his magic didn't work." She chewed her lip for a moment. "Damn. It seems like it should make sense—like we're missing something very obvious."

"All I'm missing right now is a nice warm bed," Scott said. He glanced slyly at Liz. "And maybe a little celebration of still being alive."

To his astonishment, the smile she returned was a shy one. Scott leaned back in his seat, watching the dark and deserted storefronts pass by the window, feeling surprisingly content for someone who had just had a knife held to his throat. *By God*, he thought, *there just might be a relationship brewing here.*

17

Edward Thayer kicked the end table next to the couch. The cheap pressed wood splintered, its dark veneer peeling away from the sawdust-colored material underneath. The lamp balanced precariously atop it fell to the warped floor of the houseboat, the bulb flashing brightly like a strobe before it shattered.

This place was a *dump*. When he had spoken to Reilly initially, the man had given him the impression that their old college chum Russell was a hot-shot private eye. He'd been suckered, Thayer admitted to himself. Russell had never seemed like the kind of man who might set the world on fire, but he also hadn't looked to be someone who would wind up in a floating squatter's shack. How good an investigator could he be, living like this?

Finding the place had been easy enough—he had called his office and had his secretary do it. She was probably a better detective than Scott Russell. So was the guy who changed the water bottles in the lobby, no doubt. It had taken her all of forty-five minutes to come up with the address, if you could call this floating cesspool an address. Thayer had driven his rented Mercedes to the ferry and found the houseboat less than two hours later.

His rage at losing Danny and at being hoodwinked by his old college buddy welled up again. Thayer picked up a wrought-iron chair with a torn cushion for a seat and threw it at the nearest window. The glass made a satisfying crash.

There was nothing here to tell him where Danny was, or where Russell was. No files, no paperwork except for overdue bills and junk mail piled up by the door, and no evidence than Russell did any business out of here. Perhaps the man had an office somewhere, but after seeing this place, Thayer did not for a moment believe it.

He turned toward the couch, a sprung sleeper that had possibly been a nice piece of furniture once. He squatted and hooked his fingers under its edge, then straightened, lifting the leg muscles made strong by thrice-weekly workouts. The couch was heavy but it moved, flipping over and spilling cushions. The whole boat shook as it hit the floor.

Everybody did their level best to screw him! The unions, the directors, actors, writers, they all wanted a piece of him, and once they got it, to hell with the golden goose. Now Russell had joined the crowd. The man was out there somewhere, probably drinking himself into a stupor in some sleazy bar, laughing at that fool Thayer while he spent his money.

It had been bad enough before Danny had run away, but then at least he could keep alive a faint hope that he might be able to pull the three of them together into a real family somehow. But it was impossible—the boy had never been what Thayer had hoped he would be. He was

182

weak; he had never understood that you had to take what you wanted in this world. Take it or lose it.

There had been a time, when Danny was younger, when Thayer could tell him things, could stroke his face and hair, could share with him his most private feelings. But Danny hadn't grown stronger under his father's touch—instead he had turned into a blubbering coward. That which did not destroy you was supposed to make you stronger, wasn't it?

Thayer moved to the old TV set perched on a metal bookcase between a few books. He swept the paperback volumes away, scattering them with flat slaps of his strong hands, then picked up the TV and hurled it at the overturned couch. The picture tube imploded with a loud pop as the set hit the floor, glass flying like shrapnel.

He had had enough of this shit, by God. He was going to find Russell and learn what, if anything, this ridiculous excuse for a gumshoe had managed to come up with. And he *would* bring Danny back home and teach him how to be a man. He had always gotten what he wanted from his son, and he wasn't about to stop being in control now.

It wasn't so important *why* he had to find Danny.

What was important was that it happen.

When he finished trashing Russell's houseboat, Thayer felt somewhat better. He stalked back up the dock toward his car, ignoring the stares of the people in the boats moored all about. They meant nothing. He had produced a picture that brought in sixty million domestic against a cost of less than thirty; he was somebody with clout, no mistake about that. These clowns couldn't drum up a thousand bucks free cash if ten of them chipped in. And money was only one kind of power; there were other kinds.

He was tired of being jacked around. Let somebody

else pay for a change. He hadn't always been a rich man with others doing his legwork for him. He had been a soldier, once. He knew how to wage war.

IF THE RELATIONSHIP WASN'T quite brewing to perfection, at least the coffee was.

Scott watched Liz putter away at the tiny four-burner stove in the cramped kitchen. She had swept several cartons of leftover clotted Chinese food into the garbage can, itself nearly overflowing, so the table was empty. He sat with his elbows propped on the greasy Formica, gazing at her, feeling uneasiness coil in some dark pit of his midriff.

"I might not cook for sour owl shit," she said, "but I learned a long time ago that good coffee is worth its weight in platinum."

She had a glass pot full of water bubbling on the left front burner, and when she poured it through the Melitta the aroma of the freshly ground coffee filled the air. Scott had always thought that coffee, even gourmet coffee, smelled a lot better than it tasted, but it was, after all, a cheap drug and could sometimes replace food if you drank enough of it.

"You know where the gas shutoff valve is?" he asked.

"Of course. Is there anybody in San Francisco who doesn't? Mine is behind the stove, the main is in the basement by the storage closet, and the nearest outside cutoff is on the west side of the building. You want cream or sugar?"

"Black is fine."

She put the coffee in front of him, grabbed another cup for herself and sat down. "They say caffeine makes your brain work better." She sipped at the hot brew.

Scott sighed. "God, I hope so. Our one lead to Danny

just went into the toilet. It's a big town." He blew at the steaming liquid, enjoying the smell.

Liz dropped her voice and affected a lisp. "So, shamus, what's your next move?"

"You do a lousy Bogart."

"My Mae West is better."

Scott grinned and tasted the coffee. It was pretty good as coffee went, and it certainly did a good job of blunting the chill air's edge. "Mmm. Well, to tell you the truth, I haven't got a clue. We could hang around the hotel, where the guy with the switchblade will probably want another twenty every day to keep from carving me into a jack-o'-lantern. Who knows? Maybe Danny'll come back."

"Sure, and maybe I'll win the lottery too."

He shrugged. "You're the expert on nutso types. The kid lives in a fantasy world; he really *believes* in magic, if that cop can be believed. You deal with these people all the time."

"I don't deal with them; I write about them. There's a big difference."

"Take it easy. I wasn't trying to slur your good name and professional acumen."

Liz grinned somewhat reluctantly as she poured her second cup of coffee. "You do have a certain oafish charm, you know."

"I'm trying to convince you to do your Mae West imitation again."

"Can we get serious for a second?"

He nodded. "Sure."

"What is it you think Danny's after?"

Scott surprised himself with his answer. "He's looking for the way home." As he said it, he knew, somehow, that it was true.

She frowned. "L.A. isn't that hard to find—"

"Don't play dense, Liz. You know what I mean. After all that babbling I did about peace and love and the moldering corpse of the Sixties, you know exactly what I mean. Maybe Woodstock was the pits, but the energy around the whole thing was something very important. A lot of guys my age or a little older would chuck their yuppie jobs and Beamers in a New York second if they thought they could get that feeling back and hold on to it."

Liz nodded slowly, her gaze fixed for a moment on faraway landscapes. "Yeah. Y'know, for a brief moment back then, I thought I was gonna be a real reporter. You woke that sleeping dog up again with your fairy tale."

"Are you sorry I did?"

Her gaze snapped back to him, bright and diamond-hard as usual. "I don't know. Maybe. I guess we'll see, won't we?"

"I guess we will." There was a moment of awkward silence, into which Scott plunged with: "Anyway, I think that Danny wants his fairyland as badly as old hippies want the Sixties, or maybe like Glenn Miller fans want the Forties. I guess wherever you are when you still believe in truth and justice and the American way is the place you look back on as home. I think that's what he wants. Given what I remember of his old man, Danny probably didn't get a lot of magic in his upbringing."

Liz got up and turned to the stove for the pot. *Jesus,* Scott thought, *that's her third cup. Have to peel her off the ceiling soon.* "I wouldn't think he'd find much magic on the streets panhandling or hustling."

"Granted. So where *would* he go to find it?"

She set her cup down a little too sharply; brown liquid splashed on the table. "Like I said before, it feels like we're missing something very obvious. I don't like it! I hate being one piece shy of a puzzle."

186

"I can sympathize. Maybe we need to just back off for a while, let the subconscious work on it." He smiled what he hoped was a smile full of boyish charm and said, "How's about you show me that Mae West imitation now?"

Instead of smiling back, Liz stood and went to the window, staring out at the gray sky. "I don't think it's a real good time for that now."

Scott could have sworn he felt the room vibrate as her barriers thudded into place. "Okay," he said carefully, "then I guess I'll see what's on TV, if that's okay with you."

Her shrug defined the word "noncommittal." Scott left the kitchen, which seemed to have grown perceptibly cooler despite the near-scalding coffee he had downed.

What had he done *wrong*? he asked himself repeatedly and futilely as he sat bathed in the flickering light from the tube. There seemed to be no pattern, no reason to Liz's moodiness. Even when she was friendly, however—even when she was participating in activities that are about as friendly as two people can get—there was always that substratum of reserve that could not be gotten through. He felt that she had let him in further than she had let anyone else in quite a while, but he still had not glimpsed her core.

He wondered somewhat gloomily if he ever would.

SEVEN STORIES ABOVE THE city, Edward Thayer glared at the gathering darkness. An early night-fog had begun to roll in, obscuring the waterfront like damp gray smoke and dimming the tiny jewel-like lights far below.

He didn't like this town—had never liked it. He didn't much like L.A., for that matter; it was always too dry when the Santa Anas blew, too smoggy when they didn't, too monochromatically sunshiny either way. Stop the water and the whole place would be reclaimed by the desert in a few years, nothing but sand and dust and, except for the

187

movies, good riddance. If it weren't for the money and the power to be found there he'd move to some place like New England, where they had real weather.

He was not sure of his next move, and he did not like the feeling. Should he hire another investigator—a real one, this time? It seemed prudent to find Russell first, to learn how much, if anything, he knew—but he hated waiting. Thayer was not a man who enjoyed doing nothing—

There was a knock at his door. About damned time room service got here with his dinner; it had been nearly half an hour since he called. He went to the door and jerked it open.

To his astonishment, instead of a bellboy with the dinner cart a girl stood there, a street kid with long, unwashed hair, scruffy clothes hidden under a Navy pea coat, and a dirty face. She might go fourteen, fifteen, he figured.

"What the hell do you want?"

"You're Edward Thayer," the girl said. Her voice was street-tough, her expression very nearly a sneer. She reminded him of a Saigon whore he had once had.

"Yeah, I know who I am. Whatever you're selling, I'm not buying any." He started to close the door. What kind of bullshit hotel was this, they let the riffraff come in off the street and panhandle the rooms—

"How about Danny?"

Thayer yanked the door wide. *"What?"*

"Your son. You remember, his name is Danny."

Thayer grabbed her arm and yanked her inside the room, closing the door. "I don't need smartass, girl. What are you talking about? Did Russell send you?"

She seemed oddly unafraid, even though he was towering over her. Her attitude served to increase his

188

anger. She said matter-of-factly, "I can take you to your son, Mr. Thayer. I know where he is."

"How did you find me here?"

She smiled briefly. "Magic."

He leveled a finger at her. "I told you—watch your mouth, or I'll—"

She interrupted. "Do you want Danny or not?"

Thayer rubbed at his chin, took a deep breath, and considered the situation. He could not afford to turn down any lead, no matter how unlikely in appearance. "Yes. I want him."

"Then come with me. I'll take you to him."

He made his decision. "Let me get my coat." He left her standing in the hallway as he walked to the closet. He had a full-length black leather trenchcoat that his wife had given him for Christmas a couple of years back. It was usually too hot to wear in L.A., but the foggy nights here were perfect for it.

Thayer slipped the coat from the no-steal hanger, then bent to the small travel case propped on the luggage rack. Under the socks was a small pistol, a .25 Colt Junior. It wasn't a particularly powerful weapon, but it would go bang seven times and it was loaded with special ammunition that mushroomed when it hit something the consistency of human flesh. He wasn't about to go traipsing around the city after dark following some street trash without a way to protect himself. He had learned in Nam that even a small child could be dangerous, and only a fool trusted people he didn't know.

They weren't particularly fond of handguns in this town, but if he had to use the thing, he would worry about the consequences afterward. Better twelve men trying you than six men carrying you, after all.

The little automatic made hardly any bulge in his coat

189

pocket. Thayer made sure the safety was off. All he had to do was thumb the hammer back to be able to shoot.

Ready to rock and roll . . . that's what they'd said in Nam. And God helps those who help themselves, that was as close to a creed as Edward Thayer came.

He returned to the girl. "I'm ready."

She smiled at him, a look that seemed to say she knew something he didn't. Well, fine. He figured that made them even.

18

Danny did not hear the knock. He awoke to see the maid standing by the bed. "Okay if I do the bathroom?" she asked.

"Oh, uh, sure. Go ahead." He could hardly keep his eyes open, and yet it felt as though he had been asleep for a long time. He had no watch, but there was a clock next to the bed. The luminous numbers said it was 7:58 P.M. They had checked into the hotel early in the afternoon; he had eaten and showered, so he'd been out for at least five or six hours.

Danny came out of the sleep haze, suddenly afraid. The last thing he had done before he went to bed was lock the chain lock. How had the maid gotten into the room, then? The fear blossomed into full-grown panic.

Where were Robin and the others?

He jumped from the bed, not realizing he was naked until his bare feet hit the carpeted floor. Fortunately the maid was already in the bathroom and did not see him. Danny grabbed his clothes from over the radiator where he had hung them after washing them; they were still damp, but never mind that. He had to get out of here. Robin had left him, deserted him. He should have known something like that would happen.

Maybe, he thought, *maybe they just went out to get something. Maybe they're downstairs, or even on their way back up here right now.*

But what if they weren't? He had none of the glamour that Robin was always talking about. His magic did not work, and poor Shanti was proof of that. He couldn't pull on Obi-wan Kenobi trick on the desk clerk to make him think he was paying the bill. And he sure couldn't afford to get busted. They would ship him straight back to his father. On the streets Danny could run and dodge, he knew the score, but he felt trapped inside a place like this. No doubt they had hotel detectives. Without the scatterlings and their magic, Danny would be spotted in a second as somebody who did not belong.

He had to get out, *now.*

He took the stairs, afraid that he might get caught somehow in the elevator. He could move fast for short stretches, but distance wasn't his thing; after hurrying down a few flights of stairs he was winded. His footsteps echoed in the concrete stairwell, sounding hollow and much too loud. He saw nobody using the stairs, but he kept feeling nevertheless as if somebody might leap out at him from every door he passed.

Danny drew a few curious stares as he darted across the lobby, but that didn't matter. He charged through the revolving doors and was outside, the cold night air feeling warm and friendly compared to the hotel. Nobody could catch him now. He felt relieved, like a rat that has escaped an alley dog, but he was by no means happy.

What about Robin and the others? Where were they?

He looked up and down the street, but saw no sign of them. Maybe they just went for something to eat . . .

Danny cruised, checking out a couple of fast food places, but found no sign of the scatterlings. The foggy evening chilled him, laying cool hands on his damp shirt and pants and working through to the skin beneath. He had run out so fast he had forgotten his jacket. He jammed his hands into his pants pockets and hurried up the steep sidewalk. Neon signs flashed like colored lightning against the dark buildings.

He should have known Robin would take off. She was probably mad at him because he couldn't open that claptrap or whatever they called it. Patch didn't like him very much; perhaps he had talked her and the others into abandoning him.

They had given him a test, just like in school, and he had blown it like he'd blown so many others. This had been his big chance, and he had screwed it up. It wasn't a surprise, really. You couldn't trust anybody, ever.

The tears started to run down his face, and his nose stopped up as he kept walking. What was he going to do now?

He really didn't have a lot of choices. He wasn't going back to L.A.; better to dive off the Oakland Bridge. Roberto might be pissed at him, but probably he would let him come back. Danny huddled in a doorway and considered it. He could give Roberto a story about being picked up by the cops or something. Maybe Roberto would buy that. It was worth a try, anyhow. And he could be real nice to Roberto—he knew what the older boy liked.

It was not as if he had anywhere else to go . . .

JUST AFTER THE SUN began its morning journey, Craig arose and ate a light breakfast, then prepared for his stint at Alice's bookstore.

It had been a long time since he had done an

193

autograph party. He would have preferred not to recall the last one, but alas, that occasion was one of the ugly peaks that loomed quite visibly out of the fog of drunken memory. He had been at one of the chain stores, B. Dalton's or Waldenbooks—what was it, five or six years ago?—a time, at any rate, when there had been one of those periodic resurgences of interest in photography. It had been near Christmastime, and he had gone with the honest intention of smiling at the customers and signing the books. And he had been sober. He had dressed the part, all tweeds and elbow patches and bon vivant attitude.

He had arrived a bit early and learned that they weren't quite ready for him, so he had tried to stroll leisurely along the mall. Such a thing was impossible in the pre-Christmas bustle. Were he Mephistopheles, Craig would construct a mall during Christmas shopping season somewhere about the Seventh Level of Hell to punish the most wicked of sinners. It was, quite simply, overwhelming. The shoppers stampeded along like lemmings, and there was a frantic lust permeating the air. Christmas Muzak blared, squirming children lined up to visit Santa Claus, and Craig began to feel quite claustrophobic. He tried to shake it off, but it was no use. The crowds made him want to hide, to get as far away from them as he could.

Unfortunately, there had been a liquor store in the mall, not more than a few hundred yards away from the table that the bookstore had set up for him. Into this haven from the holiday madness Craig fled, and he bought a fifth of good single-malt, clutching it to him like the salvation it was. Just a few sips should settle him down enough to make it through the rest of the evening.

A few sips in the bathroom stall did indeed greatly ease his tension. A few more sips made him downright

194

tolerant of the whole season. A few more sips, and he was beyond worry altogether, full of the spirit and of the spirit was he full . . .

He had been a little late returning to the bookstore. He felt a great deal of warmth and friendliness toward those who had come to buy his collections of pictures, and when the autographing began, he made clever jokes with the patrons. One young woman in particular seemed in awe of him, and Craig was trying—subtly, of course—to learn her phone number when, in one of the few times this had ever happened, the fine scotch rebelled and exited his system rather abruptly, ruining her dress and several hundred dollars' worth of his own work.

No, not a pleasant memory. And only one of many scenes entirely too similar. Craig still had the good grace to feel ashamed when they came back to haunt him.

Such a debacle would *not* happen today. He would eschew any thoughts of drink; he owed that much to Alice. He had his Mont Blanc pen, filled with that special teal-colored ink he fancied. He had showered, shaved, combed his hair, and found one of his better double-breasted suits that the moths had somehow overlooked. He admired himself in the hall mirror. Given his history, he still cut a rather dashing figure. Alice would approve, and Craig found that thought oddly cheering. It had been a long time since he had much cared what anyone thought of him, and it rather surprised him.

The rekindling of his interest in Faerie had awakened other dormant parts of him, perhaps. Truth was sometimes like what the headwaiter said about gentlemen: somewhat difficult to define, but he knew one when he saw one. There was something in that fictional book, *The City Under the Hill,* with the ring of truth about it. In some odd way, it gave him new hope.

195

What was the world coming to, that Douglas Craig might find some sliver of that missing quality still in his life?

SCOTT AWOKE, SAT UP, scratched at his beard stubble, and looked around. Liz was nowhere to be seen. After wending his way through mounds of semi-sorted laundry to the bathroom to deal with a pressing need, he pulled on his underwear and headed for the kitchen, led by the smell of coffee. She sat at the table, sipping a cup. He caught a glimpse of a cat's tail vanishing under the table; it moved so quickly he couldn't be sure he saw it.

"Good morning," he said. "You got a spare razor I can use?"

"Under the bathroom sink." Her voice was cool. The walls were still there; he could almost see them. He turned to go, hesitated and asked, "You okay?"

"Fine," she said. But he knew better. He had not exactly led the life of Lothario before he met her, but Scott had had enough experience to know that the word "fine," when spoken in that tone of voice, meant otherwise. He stood there for a second, feeling fat and out of shape, wondering if he should push it. *No,* he decided. *If she says she's fine, then I'll accept that. If there's something on her mind, it's her problem. Let her bring it up.*

Scott took a quick shower. The bathroom was obviously a woman's: the soap was a half cake of aromatic pink with a couple of pubic hairs embedded in it; the shampoo and deodorant were aimed at female buyers; and the pantyhose and box of tampons and hair dryer completed the picture. It struck him, somehow, as a little bit off; he had not thought of Liz as quite so feminine. Not that she wasn't female—he could testify with fair assurance to that,

196

but somehow the bathroom seemed a little on the frilly side for her. He liked it.

He liked *her* as well, quite a bit, and that bothered him more than a little. It was pretty obvious that she was gun-shy. They had not made love last night; her signals that she wanted just to sleep were subtle but unmistakable.

It was okay, though. This was someone he didn't mind sleeping, just sleeping, with. Someone he could see sleeping with, and being awake with, for quite some time.

Careful, he cautioned himself. He knew he had a tendency to rush into relationships. Just a couple of days ago he was wanting to push this woman in front of a trolley, and now he was musing about shacking up with her. *Careful, be very careful . . .*

As he toweled himself dry with the thick pink towel, Scott thought about it. There might be more here. But did he want to push it? Getting involved with somebody else had always left him worse off at the end than in the beginning. Living alone had its problems, but at least they were familiar problems. He had learned how to deal with them over the years. Lovers had to be accommodated, they wanted things over and above sex. Scott had tried and failed to find the way to give those things more than once. Each time was harder to live with afterward than the one before. Maybe the gods were trying to tell him that he was destined to be a loner.

"You about done in there?" Liz called. "I hope you left me some hot water."

He grinned. Already she was asking for stuff. Of course, it was her apartment . . .

"Be out in a second." He let himself enjoy the domesticity of the conversation—it was oddly comforting.

197

LIZ LET SCOTT FIX them some eggs and toast, and they both drank two more cups of coffee as they dawdled over breakfast.

She watched him covertly as he pushed his eggs around his plate. She was aware of the slight tension between them, and she knew he was also. For the life of her, she could not put her finger exactly on what was causing her unease. Things just seemed to be happening too fast, and Liz knew she was as much to blame as he was.

It had been over two years since she had lived with anyone, and that had not ended well. An interoffice romance—never a good idea to begin with—her romantic entanglement with Sean, otherwise now and forever identified in her mind as the Artiste, had been a disaster from the first day. He had been a fascinating personality—a copywriter not wholly without talent, though not nearly as good as he thought he was. He had had aspirations of being a novelist, and to that end had been building a novel for the past five years the way some men who live in the desert build boats—carefully tinkering with the engine and polishing the woodwork and brass, but never finishing it.

Unfortunately, he had also been of the opinion that his artistic bent gave him license to be a complete and utter asshole toward other people. Liz had put up with his angst-ridden neuroses for the better part of six months, and why she had stood for it that long she never did figure out. But one day she had finally overcome the inertia of the relationship and moved out.

She had thought she had gotten over it fairly quickly, had even been considering, for the past few months, looking about for Someone New. But now that the possibility had presented itself, she was not so sure it was a good idea. Not that she didn't like Scott—she did. She found him attractive, reasonably good in bed, and no more untidy than she was, which admittedly was not saying much. And he had respected her request to not push her toward something she wasn't sure she wanted.

So what was the problem here?

Maybe—though she hated to admit it—she was still looking for some kind of pyrotechnic epiphany. A celestial sign that would inform her in no uncertain terms that this was The One. *Well, good luck, girl,* Liz thought. *Remember that God's a man—He's on their side.*

The silence was getting too thick and heavy for her. "So, you come up with any brilliant ideas about finding Danny?" she asked.

Scott shrugged. "I guess our only bet is to go back to the Larkspur and see if he shows up, much as I hate to suggest it. Maybe somebody else there knows him."

"I can't stay on this story forever," Liz said. "If we don't get something going pretty soon, I'll have to run with what I've got."

"Without knowing the end?"

"Listen, I can do Hitchcock endings in my sleep. Real poignant stuff, kids wandering the mean streets, fairy godmothers masquerading as bag ladies. We don't do Ibsen in my biz."

"That's for sure," he muttered.

She glared at him, and he looked apologetic. This was something they hadn't resolved, and would surely have to if there was a chance in hell of this relationship, or whatever it was, proceeding: his attitude toward her work. It was all right for her to denigrate it, but woe betide anyone else who did so, especially someone whom she had let get close to her.

199

The silence returned, thick as bay fog, rolling in between them.

THE LARKSPUR WAS NO more appealing a place to be than it had been yesterday. Scott had Liz park where they could watch the main entrance to the boarded-up fleabag, but far enough away that the Latino rough trade with the knife probably would not happen across them accidentally. He wished he had kept the cheap binoculars he had bought when he was working for the agency, but another op had offered him thirty bucks for them, and the money had looked very good at the time. He had prepared a little something in the way of self-defense, however. In his shirt pocket was half a plastic straw filled with red pepper from Liz's kitchen. The ends of the striped tube were stoppered with little wads of paper. Scott had seen the trick while watching some late-night spy movie on cable. The idea was to use the thing like a pea shooter and blast your assailant's eyes full of pepper. Same principle as Mace—at least, so the guy in the movie had said.

Whether Scott would have the nerve to blow pepper into the face of someone holding a switchblade on him was by no means a foregone conclusion, but at least he would have the option. He had gotten a few grains of the spice in his eyes and nose before, and judging by his reaction he figured anybody with a face full of it all at once would have other things to do than worry about than sticking him with a cheap Italian blade.

"Exciting work, being a private detective," Liz said, breaking in on his thoughts.

"Ain't it? You'd be a natural at it, though. You've already obeyed the first rule of surveillance."

"What's that?"

"Always park in the shade."

She laughed. It made him feel good to know that he could make her laugh.

IT WAS NEARLY NOON, and the shade of the building in which they had parked the Toyota had moved. San Francisco wasn't like Phoenix or L.A., to be sure, but it wasn't Alaska either, and the sun was making the interior of the car uncomfortably warm.

Liz squirmed uncomfortably. "I have to pee," she said. "What's it say in the detective rulebook about that?"

"Well, it's easier for guys. We usually carry an old plastic soft-drink bottle, one of the big ones, and just drain and fill as needed."

She stared at him in disbelief. "I haven't tried to pee into a bottle since I was five. It didn't work then and I have no reason to believe it'll work now."

He carefully kept the smile he felt from showing. "We could go find a gas station. Or you could walk over there behind that abandoned sofa. Nobody'd see you there."

She pulled one foot up under her, sitting on it. "You really know how to show a girl a good time, don't you?"

"Just trying to be helpful— Hello?" He sat up, staring through the windshield.

"What?"

Scott pointed, trying to keep from becoming too excited. "Look at that kid coming up the street. Doesn't that look like—?"

Liz grabbed the picture of Danny from the sun visor and glanced at it, then back at the teenager approaching. The boy looked around warily, then stepped through one of the cut-out sections in the fence and moved toward the front of the Larkspur.

"It's him!" she said in astonishment. "Jesus, talk about luck! Okay, so what do we do now?"

201

"Now we wait."

"We could go in after him—"

"Yeah, and run into the entire cast of *West Side Story*, maybe. No, let's sit tight. Sooner or later he'll come out." Scott grinned, feeling a quiet glow of pride. He had done it, just like a real detective. Maybe, just maybe, he had a future in this business after all.

19

Nothing had changed in the shabby room that Danny could see. Roberto was sprawled on one of the mattresses, wearing jeans but no shirt, his eyes vacant, bloodshot. Birdclaw must have scored some dope from somewhere, Danny realized; the burned-leaf smell of weed was thick in the air and Roberto certainly didn't appear to be feeling any pain. That was good; usually Roberto was pretty mellow when he was stoned—unless he had been drinking as well. He was a mean drunk, and a few joints seldom cooled him out much.

He found out rather swiftly that Roberto must have had a few beers, because the older boy certainly wasn't happy to see him. "Where you been, you little punk? Huh? Where the *fuck* you been? You don't just take off without telling me, man, you just don't *do* that!"

Danny flashed a nervous grin, trying not to show the sudden fear he felt. "Hey, I'm sorry, but it's like, it wasn't my fault. I—I was hustling tourists for change and the cops grabbed me, y'know?"

Roberto stared right through him. "Yeah? So why ain't you in jail, asshole?"

Danny sat down on the weight bench, thinking furiously. "I—I got away. They let me go to the toilet and I climbed out through the window."

"Bullshit."

"No, it's true, I swear!"

Roberto lurched to his feet, weaving slightly. He bent over and glared at Danny, who could smell the liquor on his breath. This was going to be bad. "I don't think so. You know what I think? I think maybe you started turning tricks."

"C'mon, 'Berto, you know I'm not into that."

"That's what *you* say. But yesterday some old shit was parked out front lookin' for you. He gave me some money—money he said he owed you. Now what the hell would anybody owe *you* money for, Danny boy? You ain't got but one thing you can sell." Roberto slapped Danny, lightly, but enough to sting. The boy flinched away from it. "He had a woman with him, too. Real kinky stuff, huh?"

Danny was starting to feel frantic now. "I don't know what you're talkin' about! I didn't turn any tricks. Nobody owes me money."

Roberto swaggered over to his weights. When he was stoned, Danny remembered, he often got into working out fairly heavily. He worked his arms and back and chest a lot, but he never worked his legs. They didn't show, he told Danny once, so what was the point?

He picked up the barbell, which had at least sixty or seventy pounds on it, and began to do curls. He moved the iron quickly, pumping out rep after rep. "It's okay," he said, finishing his set of curls. He shifted his grip without putting down the weight and began a series of overhead presses. "Now that you're selling your ass, maybe we can make some decent money."

"I ain't selling it, I swear! You never wanted me to—"

Roberto put the weights down and glared at Danny. "Well, I changed my mind. Who gives a shit about gettin' AIDS, anyway? Life ain't that good." He was looking quite pumped from his workout, his arms swollen and hard, his face flushed. "You can start payin' your way, or you can vamoose, amigo—you understand? Go find somebody else to take care of you. I can pick from a hundred punks like you, you ain't worth nothin'."

It was bad—very bad. Danny tried to keep his breathing from revealing his panic. "Roberto, he said, softly, persuasively, the same tone he had used so often on his father (*and which had never worked*), "hey, c'mon, man, you're my friend. Please—"

"*Nobody* walks out on me and comes back, not without paying for it. You're on the streets, shithead. You don't like it, you don't live here no more."

He turned toward Danny. "G'wan. You get out, *now*, or I'll stomp your butt into hamburger!"

Danny knew how serious this was. Roberto had a mean streak. Most of the time Danny had been able to get around it by talk or sex, but at the moment the bigger boy was between him and the door. The only course was to boogie, perhaps try again later when Roberto was straight.

"Okay, I'm goin', I'm goin'. Chill out, okay?" Danny spread his hands wide to indicate how harmless he was. But somehow it was the wrong thing to do. Instead of being pacified, Roberto got even more angry.

"You think I'm gonna let you off that easy, you lyin' little turd? You cocksucking *punk*! I'm gonna teach you to lie to me!"

Danny looked frantically around the room for help,

205

for a way out, for anything. He would never make it past Roberto. He remembered seeing the older boy lay into a wino once. Roberto had broken the guy's ribs and arms and knocked out what few teeth were left in the sodden, whiskered face. And had laughed during it.

Danny knew what was going to happen. He was dead meat.

"Hey, man, no, *please,* I'll do anything you want. I'll go on the streets and hook, anything you want . . ."

He was babbling, he knew, because it did not matter what he said now—it was too late. Roberto wanted blood, he wanted to use those muscles, and Danny was the only target within sight.

Danny darted to one side, trying to get around the stoned menace. If he could make it to the hall—

Roberto stuck his foot out and tripped him. Danny sprawled on the filthy floor. He rolled, tried to come up on his feet, but was a shade too slow. A hard fist caught him on the side, low on the ribs, as he scrambled on his hands and knees. He cried out.

Another punch landed, high on his back. Danny twisted and scrambled to his feet, but Roberto was already at the door, blocking it.

"Come on, punk! *Come on!* You want a piece'a me? I sure as shit want one'a you!"

Danny backpedaled. His left heel hit something on the floor and he almost tripped and fell again. He glanced down; it was one of Roberto's weights, a small one weighing perhaps two pounds. Without thinking, Danny snatched up the plastic-coated concrete, held it cocked like a stone.

Roberto laughed. "You think you can hit me with that?"

At that instant Danny wasn't sure what he intended,

but Roberto's taunt was enough to trigger him. He heaved the weight. The distance was perhaps twelve feet; Roberto twisted, trying to maneuver out of the way, not entirely successfully. The weight hit him on the upper arm, right at the shoulder. It must have hurt, but the thick muscle there kept it from doing any real damage. Its only result was to enrage Roberto even more.

"I'm gonna *kill* you for that! You're dead! You're history!" He charged, spittle flying from his mouth.

Danny's bowels clenched as though suddenly packed with ice. Roberto *would* kill him. He was going to die, here and now! The fear washed over him, filling him to his core, immobilizing him like a rabbit transfixed by approaching headlights. Danny went blank, became a mindless thing waiting to die.

Within that deepest frozen core, a spark glowed.

The barbell with which Roberto had been working leaped from the floor as though snatched up by an invisible giant. The heavy weight sailed through the air as Roberto came to an abrupt stop, his drugged eyes going wide in the instant before the metal bar caught him across the throat, clotheslining him. His head snapped back and he was smashed into the floor, the weights on the ends of the bar sinking into the worn linoleum as though it were soft sand, burying the weights fully half their diameter.

The bar crushed Roberto's throat, pinning him to the floor. He thrashed his legs, hooked his hands under the thick metal, trying to shove the weight away. But his strength, which had lifted it repeatedly just a few moments before, could not budge it now.

Danny watched in detached fascination as Roberto gurgled, his face turning purple. His arms and legs thrashed more spasmodically now. A sudden smell, like the bathroom down in the lobby that the winos used,

207

caused Danny's nose to wrinkle. He saw a dark stain spread down Roberto's jeans.

After a few more seconds Roberto stopped thrashing. And stopped breathing.

Danny stared at the body, feeling suddenly drained and exhausted. It did not stop an adrenal surge as he realized what had happened, however. Roberto was dead!

Danny did what he always did when faced with something he could not deal with. He turned and ran.

LIZ AND SCOTT APPROACHED the front of the fenced building. Liz made a face as she noticed the smell of stale urine in the warm air. "I'd feel a lot better if you had a gun," she said.

"I doubt it," Scott replied. "I'd be just as likely to shoot you or myself as anybody else if it came down to it. I know squat about guns; that's movie stuff. I don't even know anybody who's got a concealed weapons permit."

Liz looked around. There was not much traffic, either on the street or the sidewalks, and the few people who were in sight had a definite seedy appearance. There were five teenagers strolling toward then, four boys and a girl, all looking like they had been outfitted by the Salvation Army. Liz wondered uneasily if they might be part of a gang. That was all they needed at this point.

Calm down, she thought. She could take care of herself if push came to shove. A sharp fingernail in the eye or a knee to the *cojones* would give a mugger something to think about while she made fast tracks elsewhere. She wasn't foolish enough to wear high heels on the streets; her track shoes would carry her at a good clip if the need arose. She only hoped Scott also knew when to hold 'em and when to fold 'em . . .

They had reached the rusty chain-link fence supported by chunks of concrete, and were about to step through one of the holes in it when the front door of the hotel suddenly burst open. Danny Thayer came tearing out, running for all he was worth. He didn't slow as he saw them, he just flew past as if all the demons in Hell were on his tail.

Liz saw Scott freeze, apparently too surprised to try to stop the boy. Danny darted through the hole in the fence and sprinted toward the street. Liz ran after him. "Come on!" she yelled over her shoulder.

As Danny ran across the street, Liz noticed that the teenagers she had seen coming up the walk also began to run, angling across the street and following Danny. She didn't have time to worry about that, however; the way the kid was moving he would be out of sight in a few seconds.

Scott passed her, moving pretty well for a guy as out of shape as he'd appeared when naked. Liz nearly lost her purse as she jumped over an overturned garbage can, but managed to grab it in one hand as she dodged a derelict sprawled on the sidewalk.

Up ahead, Danny turned into a narrow side street. The five teenagers were right behind him. Who were they? she wondered. Friends of Danny's, perhaps?

Scott was breathing hard enough for Liz to hear him as they entered the street, which seemed to Liz more like a glorified alley. They ran past an overflowing dumpster, its stink of rotted garbage high in the air. Liz stepped in something that squished; she slid a hair to one side, but managed to keep her footing. She didn't want to think about what it might have been.

The street made an L-turn to the left, and she glimpsed Danny rounding it. The others were right behind him. Liz passed Scott, whose wind had finally given out.

209

He was a few feet behind her, breathing hard enough to make her glad that she had had CPR training.

Liz reached the new corridor, slowing as she did so on the chance that someone might be waiting for her around the bend.

She came around the corner. The pavement continued for perhaps another hundred feet, then ended against the wall of a building. What she saw made her skid to an abrupt halt. Scott huffed his way around the corner behind her and stopped as well. They both stared in disbelief.

There was nobody there.

The street was a dead end, with no other way out. But Danny and his five pursuers were gone, as though the earth had opened up and swallowed them.

"WELL," SCOTT SAID, SITTING down somewhat precariously on a standpipe that jutted from the brick wall, "it beats the hell out of me."

They had gone over the length of the street twice. There was simply no way out other than past them. No doors or windows at ground level. There was a fire escape ladder running down one side of the building, and Scott had moved a trash can under it and pulled it down. The rusty steel had loudly protested the move, and it had taken all his weight to lower the ladder—it obviously had not been moved in years. Scott had climbed up to the only window, a square of chicken-wire-reinforced glass and wood perhaps thirty feet up. He had tried to open it, but it was locked, and he could see that the lock had been painted shut long ago. A thick patina of dust coated both the sill and the window. Even if Danny and his mysterious pursuers had somehow managed to pull the ladder down without it being heard—impossible, since they were only out of sight for a few seconds—there was no way they could have gotten into the building.

That was the bottom line—there was no way in hell that those six kids could have done what they had done. Nowhere to hide, nothing but blank walls and trash cans, all of which were filled with garbage.

"This is getting mondo weird," Liz said. "It's like . . . like—"

"Like magic," Scott said softly.

She looked at him. "Come *on*. I might buy hypnosis or drugs, unlikely as those are, but—"

He looked at her; his expression, she thought, was the sort normally associated with people who are about to begin speaking in tongues.

"Maybe it was a gallitrap," he said.

"Huh?"

"I read about them in that fantasy novel I picked up at the store. Some kind of door between dimensions or something, I think. Between Faerie and this world."

Liz was starting to feel very nervous. The walls of the cul-de-sac seemed somehow closer, and insidiously threatening. "Look, Scott—"

"We were right behind them," he said calmly. "There's no way out except the way we came. And they didn't leave that way. Did they?"

Liz reluctantly shook her head.

He stood up. "The book is at my houseboat. I think maybe we should go and get it."

"Why?"

"I think there may be some information in it that'll help us."

"I don't see how—"

He looked at her and spread his hands as though they were discussing a choice of movies to see. "Do you have any better ideas?"

She felt abruptly very tired, very weak. She did not

211

want to be dealing with any of this anymore. "It'll take us the rest of the day to get to Sausalito and back."

"I think it's important. I really do."

His calmness was somehow infuriating—as though he had suddenly become aware of a cosmic truth that was somehow soothing instead of frightening, as she found it.

"Look," Liz said, trying desperately to inject an element of rationality into the discussion, "I've got a copy at my apartment. It's closer—"

He frowned in thought. "I've got a better idea than that. Let's just go back to the bookstore where we got them. That's just a few miles from here."

Liz realized that there was no talking him out of this. "Okay, fine." She turned away. "Come on. Let's get back to my car before somebody steals the tires and puts it on blocks." She did not want to go back to the bookstore; what she wanted, more than anything else, was simply to go back to her apartment, go to bed, pull the covers over her head and pretend that none of this had ever happened. But that, unfortunately, was not an option. She could walk away from it, true enough, but she could never stop thinking about it. Never.

If Scott had suggested cutting open a chicken and looking for answers there, at this point Liz could not have posed any real objections. A hole had evidently opened up in thin air and swallowed those kids, and a similar hole—big and black and inexplicable—now yawned in her life. Something had just broken all the rules, and nothing seemed safe anymore. Liz shivered as they walked back to the main street. Though the sun was still shining, she felt as though she might never be warm again.

DANNY WAS NEVER SO happy to see anybody as he was Puck and the others, even Patch. He started to explain to

212

them about Roberto, about how the barbells had killed him by themselves, the words tumbling over each other in his haste to get them out, but Patch cut him off.

"Quiet! Move in close to us, quick!"

Danny did so, and felt a strange tingling in the air about him, like static electricity on a dry day. The brick walls of the street seemed to shimmer momentarily, as though seen through heat waves. Then his attention was distracted by the sight of the two people he had seen in front of the Larkspur coming around the corner.

He felt a momentary sense of panic, even though he and the scatterlings outnumbered them three to one—it was a knee-jerk reaction he always felt in the presence of adults. But something was odd here; the man and the woman were looking right at them, but blankly, as though they didn't see Danny and the scatterlings.

Patch took Danny's arm and led him as he and the others walked around the two, who continued to stare stupidly at the empty dead end. They walked quickly back toward the street. "More magic," Danny said in realization. "You made us invisible!"

"To them, yes. Step it up—we've got to hurry. Tonight is Walpurgis E'en."

Danny nodded, not really understanding the urgency, just happy that he had not been deserted after all. "Where's Robin?"

He saw them glance at each other. "On an errand," Lull said softly.

They hurried up the street, Danny's heart buoyant enough to almost make him float. They had not deserted him after all! If he had not panicked back in the hotel room they would no doubt have come back for him. He still had a chance to enter Faerie.

"Who were those two chasing you?" Puck asked.

213

Danny shrugged. "Don't know; I never saw 'em before. Roberto"—Jesus, Roberto was *dead!*—"Roberto said there was a guy lookin' for me yesterday. Maybe somebody my father sent or something." The fear crept back into his speech; his voice nearly cracked when he spoke of his father. To change the subject, he asked, "Where are we going?"

Random said, "To see if you are really the Keymaster, as Robin thinks."

"I . . . I couldn't do it before. Why would it be any different now?"

He had asked the question of Patch, who scowled blackly and did not reply. Puck grinned, and something in his look gave Danny a chill. "It will be. You'll see."

20

There were not, as preparations went, very many things to be done to ready the Looking Glass for a book signing. Alice had done scores of them over the last twenty years, ranging from unknown first novelists to a few authors who had regularly scaled the heights of the *New York Times Book Review*. Still, she thought as she bustled around, stacking what she hoped was an artful display of Abrams editions of Douglas's photographs upon the table he would use, it would hardly do for her not to have it ready before he arrived. There had been the other touches as well: the hand-lettered placard in the front window and the free radio spot on the public channel. There had not been time for an ad in the local booksellers' weekly; this day had been the only one open in the next month, and so it had been rather a last-minute thing.

Most writers provided their own pens, but she had several set out just in case they were needed. She set a pitcher of ice water within reach but far enough away so as to not be knocked over by the author or an adoring fan.

The signing was not to begin until eleven; it would end at one. That would allow the lunch crowd, such as it might be, a chance to see the famous photographer.

The Vivaldi tape playing in the background—the "Spring" section of his *Four Seasons*—filled the store with the sound of joyous strings. Perhaps later this evening, some other composer would be more appropriate. Ravel, perhaps? Alice smiled at herself.

In truth, she did not expect a swarm of autograph seekers for this signing, since it had been some time since Douglas had come out with a new book. There had been revised editions of some of his better-known works, a "best-of" collection having been published only a few years past, but by and large Douglas was hardly a chart-topper these days. She had to confess that her reasons for this signing had more to do with Douglas the man than they did with Craig the photographer. Mrs. Kopfman's daughter Alice had ulterior motives. It had been some years since she had felt stirred by a man as she did by Douglas. He was of her time, shaped by the same memories and forces that had shaped her. Speak to the children who came into her shop about gas rationing and meat coupons and you might as well be speaking of the Revolutionary War. These college students to whom the Sixties were ancient history could in no way relate to the Forties. They had heavy metal and rap where she had grown up with swing, and coming of age in the Eighties they took for granted things that Alice would have considered miracles in the days of victory gardens and scrap-metal drives. She glanced at the computer on her desk.

But Douglas shared these memories with her. When he had asked her to dine with him and then agreed to the autographing, her heart had fluttered. Alice chuckled at herself. She did not regret that the world had moved on—that was the way of things—but she could be forgiven

216

for wishing to be with someone whose roots were sunk as deeply as were her own. She did not think of herself as one who lived in the past, but neither could she pretend the same interest in the future as she had once had.

There were no customers in the shop at the moment, so Alice took a moment to slip into the bathroom and look at her hair in the mirror. She brushed a few stray strands back into place, then checked her face. She had used a touch of makeup this morning to brighten her cheeks a bit, and had worn her favorite gray sweater over her pale blue silk blouse and darker blue skirt. She smiled at her image in the mirror, and the lines at the corners of her eyes deepened. She had never been a beauty, but she had always taken care to be neat, and if Father Time had laid his weathering hands upon her, he had not yet turned her sloppy in her habits. She liked Douglas, and she liked looking nice for him. She felt very much at peace on this sunny day; the only small bit of sorrow she felt was that Mao was still missing. She had reluctantly come to the conclusion that the cat would not be returning . . .

The sound of the front door opening broke into her thoughts, and she turned away from the mirror. Perhaps Douglas had arrived early?

DANNY FOLLOWED THE SCATTERLINGS into the bookstore, glancing around with an emotion akin to relief. This was a familiar place. He didn't read all that well, but there were plenty of books here with pictures in them, and he knew that some of the older ones had neat engravings in black and white. Besides, he liked this bookstore, liked the musty smell of old paper and the pleasant untidiness to it.

He saw a copy of a large book with a photograph on the cover that he recognized as the same as the poster he had on his wall. He had leafed through a copy of that book before, but none of the other pictures in it had been of Fairyland, and so he had not been interested. He had always wondered if that was really a picture of Fairyland. It would be nice to think that that was the way it looked.

A thought occurred to him. There was only one reason for them to bring him here, after all. "You mean . . . it's in *here*?" Danny asked. "The gallitrap?"

"One of them is—for all the good it does us," Random said.

"So where's Robin?"

"Not here yet," Lull said. "It's not time. She'll be here pretty soon." She gestured toward the downstairs section. "We'll wait for her down there."

Danny followed the scatterlings. He felt excited, though he wasn't sure why. There was something in the air, some kind of . . . energy that made his skin crawl, though the sensation was not unpleasant. It grew stronger as they went down the stairs. He wondered if it had anything to do with tonight being—what had Robin called it? Walpurgis Eve.

He shrugged. All that really mattered was that Robin would be here soon. And when she arrived, everything would be okay. Of that he was sure.

CRAIG ARRIVED JUST BEHIND a group of teenagers who quickly moved from his view downstairs. For a moment he thought they looked familiar, but they were gone before he could be sure. Before he could give the matter any further thought, he heard Alice call him.

"Douglas!"

She was behind her desk, beaming at him, and he felt once again that comforting earth-mother solidity that she seemed to carry with her. She looked quite nice, and he lost no time in telling her so. Her smile grew wider still. "You look rather impressive yourself," she replied. "You're early. Let me make you some tea, or perhaps coffee? We can sit and visit."

He nodded. "Yes. I would like that very much." He looked about and exhaled deeply, feeling suddenly very relaxed. Alice seemed very much a part of her store, and he realized that her comforting presence permeated the stacks of books around him as well. It was a grounding influence that required nothing of Craig other than that he be there to experience it. He realized that he felt more comfortable in this store than he had felt anywhere in quite a long time, including his favorite watering holes. He felt grateful to know that such feelings were left in him.

THAYER CAME AWAKE ABRUPTLY. He looked about, confused. The sunshine coming through a nearby window was warm on his lower body.

He sat up. He was lying on a bed in a strange hotel room, and sitting in a chair nearby, staring at him, was a thin teenaged girl. Memory returned, albeit hazily. The girl—Robin, that was her name—had offered to take him to Danny. She had said she needed to stop by her hotel room first.

Once they had entered the room he had abruptly felt exhausted. This was quite unusual for him—even though he was not as young as he used to be, he still had a lot of energy; he had to in his line of work. But he had sat down on the bed, and the last thing he remembered had been Robin's eyes as they stared fixedly at him, somehow almost luminous . . .

"What happened?" he demanded of her.

She shrugged. "You fell asleep. I tried to wake you, but you didn't seem interested. So I let you sleep."

Thayer shook his head in bafflement. This made no sense at all; he had gotten a good eight hours the night before, which was all he ever needed. For a brief moment he

219

considered the possibility that the girl might have drugged him, but discounted it immediately. He had not eaten or drunk anything with her, she surely hadn't shot him up with anything, and even granting the possibility, what motive could she have had? He checked his wallet; it was still in his hip pocket, his credit cards and cash undisturbed. The little gun was in his coat. If she had wanted to rob him he would have already been picked clean and she would have been long gone.

"What time is it?"

"Just after eleven."

He stared at her. "Good Christ, I've been asleep for almost sixteen hours!"

She nodded. He had the feeling somehow that she was amused, but her expression was quite sober. "You must have been tired."

"I guess so." He stood. "What about Danny?"

She stood up as well. "If you're ready, I'll take you to him now."

Thayer followed her from the hotel, which was a far classier place than he would have thought she could afford from her looks. He ought to know better, though; he had known rock stars and actors who looked scuzzier than her by far, and they could buy and sell whole towns if they wanted.

Something about this still felt wrong, but Thayer couldn't quite put his finger on what it was. Maybe he was just nervous about seeing Danny again. The boy was, after all, his one real failure in life. There didn't seem to be any of him in the boy, though he knew that Danny was certainly his son. His wife had been a virgin when they had met, and had gotten pregnant on their two-week honeymoon. Which was no great surprise, considering they had spent almost the entire Hawaii trip in bed. In bed, on the floor, on the lanai,

220

even on the beach under a blanket once. Three, four times a day. Estelle had been something back then, and no mistake. Thayer shook his head ruefully. Never was the same after the kid was born, though. Particularly after they moved to Los Angeles and he got involved in the industry. She had never seemed able to understand that it was a cutthroat business, that he had to be on top of things twenty-four hours a day. That was what it meant to be a provider.

All right, so he couldn't fix Estelle—it didn't mean he had to give up on Danny yet. The boy was his only child, and by God, Thayer was going to leave some imprint on him. There was no place on Earth where the boy could run that would be far enough.

But he had to be careful. Losing control the way he had in that sty of a houseboat had been a bad sign. He had to keep a tight rein on himself, hold himself steady. He hadn't gotten to be where he was today by blowing it.

Robin sat in the passenger seat of his car, giving him directions as he drove up through Chinatown. It was like a Disneyland version of Saigon. The whole city, in fact, had the same self-conscious air of pseudo-reality as a sound stage. New York, now that was a city that was real. You could walk out of some posh Upper East Side high-rise and get mugged in broad daylight. It certainly put an edge on life.

Maybe this little tramp sitting next to Thayer was right; maybe he had been more tired than he thought he was. Maybe he had only needed to sleep to recharge his batteries. He had to admit that he felt a lot better than he had since Danny had run away. This mess was almost over; pretty soon he would be able to get back to his life again.

SCOTT AND LIZ ARRIVED at the bookstore. The grandmotherly type who ran it was talking to a white-haired man who looked vaguely familiar to Scott. Both were off in

221

their own world and barely noticed him and Liz as they went down the stairs to the fantasy section.

Liz stopped partway down the stairs, frowning. "What?" Scott asked.

She looked down the aisle, then shook her head. "Nothing. For a second I thought I saw somebody."

"There's nobody down here that I can see."

"I know." She shrugged, dismissing the incident, and continued down the shelves and into an aisle of bookshelves. "Let's see, the book was over here . . ."

"I got it." Scott pulled the book from the shelf and began to flip through it. After a moment he held it out so that Liz could read over his shoulder. "Here's the section I wanted you to read."

Maeve, Queen of Faerie, stood looking through the polished quartz of the tall window in the South Tower. The view was of the gentle hills of Tir Nan Og. She felt weary. Her years weighed heavily upon her, though she showed them not. Oberon's request had not surprised her, but it had disturbed her nonetheless.

To close the gallitraps would forever sunder the connection between man's world and her own, and her mind and heart were sore troubled by that possibility.

Oberon, blast his ambitious hide, knew that enough truth lay in his words to roil the already swirling waters of her conscience. Could he be right? Were the comings and goings of the carefree and careless scatterlings in some part responsible for the discord in the Realm? Did they carry some hubretic disease from men, infecting the inhabitants of the Realm and weakening their vital essences?

She did not really think it was so, but she was Queen, and it was upon her head that the responsibility for all rested.

What was she to do? Did she dare risk the Realm on her belief that Oberon was wrong? What if he were right?

"Read this part right here," Scott said, pointing.

"I've already read it. You move your lips when you read, did you know that? Turn the page."

Maeve turned away from the window. Perhaps there was a compromise. The gallitraps at present were open to any in Faerie who chose to use them. She could restrict their use without closing them altogether; limit them so that only those of True Blood could come and go at will. If the scatterlings wished to roam the lands of men, they could continue to do so, but they would not be able to open the portals from that side. Did they but know that before they left the Realm, then that should be forewarning enough. If they wished to return, they would have to petition one of the True Blood—if they could find one—for assistance.

Oberon was correct in that the scatterlings were irresponsible. Perhaps this would teach them a needed lesson.

And with exit allowed but not re-entrance, then it could be seen if the Realm was truly being polluted by the unnatural energies that permeated the other world. If indeed the Realm grew stronger, if the bellblossoms began to sing again and the crystal mountains began to shine as brightly as they had once upon a time, then perhaps there would be something to what Oberon wished. He had other motives, of course—such intrigues and betrayals had always been the way of the Court, but that was another problem, to be solved on another day.

"Come on, turn the page," Liz said. "I'm getting old here waiting on you."

"Hold on a second, speed-reader."

The Queen summoned Oberon to the Court. Anticipation was high in the air, the sprites felt the winds of change, the omdeh huddled together in bright clumps in the corners of the vast throne room, burbling softly to themselves.

Oberon bowed before her. "My Queen."

"I have reconsidered your suggestion, Oberon. I will not close the gallitraps, but there may be some merit in restricting their usage. Therefore, here is what I have decided . . ."

She could not help but notice the gleam of triumph in his cold eyes as she spoke to him, the hint of a cruel smile playing about the corners of his mouth despite his attempt to hold it in check. Aye, Oberon was, as always, the most dangerous of her kind. Turning a careless back upon him would be a foolish act beyond compare.

She would have to watch him carefully . . .

"That seems to be it," Scott said. "The writer wanders off into a troll hunt or something in the next chapter." He closed the book and put it back on the shelf.

"So what does that tell us?" Liz asked. "You don't really believe all this crap, do you?"

He shook his head slowly. "I don't know. If you had asked me a few days ago I would have been sure it was all fantasy. Now, after Danny and those other kids vanished into thin air . . ."

"We didn't see that happen," she reminded him.

"Yeah, well, unless one of those kids was the Amazing Spider-Man in disguise, I can't see any other explanation. Come on, Liz," Scott continued as she looked like she was about to voice another objection, "you're too hardheaded a reporter, even despite all those years of made-up stories, to deny this. There was no earthly way for them to get out of that dead-end."

She nodded reluctantly. "I know. But I don't know if I'm ready to say it was because of magic."

"I'm open to a better suggestion."

It was Liz's turn to shake her head. "I was afraid you might say that." She was silent for a moment. "So now what?"

Scott chewed his lower lip for a moment. "Maybe we should check some books on magic—find out more about gallitraps."

"Oh, sure, what the hell—then we can go consult a psychic. We keep one on retainer for the *Star*." Liz turned back toward the stairs. "The mythology section's upstairs—I saw it on the way in."

WHILE THE TWO LOOKED at the book, Danny and the scatterlings stood not ten feet away from the pair, watching them, hidden by a veil of glamour.

"I don't like this," Random said nervously. "They know something. Did you see the way they were looking at old Mac Tir Wo Tosh's book?"

"They're leaving," Danny said in relief.

225

"We ought to be sure," Puck said. "I'll follow them, make sure they leave. We don't want any problems now."

Puck started up the stairs after the couple. Patch, Random, Lull and Pinch stayed with Danny. Patch turned to look at Danny. He seemed afraid, but of what, Danny had no idea. Surely not of him . . .

"Can you see it?" the scatterling asked Danny.

Danny was about to reply "See what?" but something made him hold his tongue. He turned and looked about the basement floor. That tingling in the air was stronger than ever now. He remembered that he had felt it before, in the tunnel beneath the street a few days ago . . .

At the far end of the aisle the air seemed to shimmer slightly, as though he could glimpse a light from a great distance. "There," he said, pointing.

The scatterlings looked at each other in astonishment—and, in Patch's case, nervousness. "Robin was right," Lull said. "He *is* a changeling."

"That was never in doubt," Patch said.

"I'm a—*what?*"

Patch wheeled toward him, anger naked in his expression now. Danny took an involuntary step backward. "You fool," the scatterling hissed. "You're a *sibhreach*, a switched baby! Somebody from the Realm changed you for a human child right after you both were born. Changelings are usually gross and stupid, and the Lady knows you fit that part—and they almost never remember who they really are."

Danny felt suddenly dizzy. He was right—all along, he had been right! "Y-you mean I was born in Fairyland?"

"Yes, for all the good it'll do you. Your birthright will be your death warrant!"

Pinch grabbed his arm. "You can't tell him—"

"Yes, I can! Returning to the Realm is a bad idea—I've said so all along!" He turned back to Danny. "Robin'll do

226

anything to go home, round-ears. If she has to, she'll feed you to a demon, the worst monster you can imagine! If that's what it takes to open the gallitrap, then that's what she'll do!"

"I don't believe you! Robin wouldn't do that!"

"It may already be too late! Believe me, she wants to go home in the worst way, ever since Queen Maeve sealed the way of return to us. You can't believe she cares anything for you!"

"Don't listen to him!" Lull said to Danny. "If you want to return to Faerie with us, you must open the gallitrap! Robin will be here soon, and we can all go home!"

"Yes," Patch said, and the fire he had worn when Danny first saw him was on him again now, blazing along the seams of his jacket, running like electricity in slow motion down his arms. "Yes, but at what price? At the sacrifice of one of True Blood? Have you any idea what they'll *do* to us for that?"

The four scatterlings were all shouting at each other now. Danny staggered away from them, his mind whirling with fragmented thoughts and fears. Could it be? Was he about to be betrayed after all? Would Robin—beautiful Robin, his Robin—willingly sacrifice him?

There was only one response possible to him—the same knee-jerk reaction he had operated on unquestioningly for years. Without speaking, Danny twisted around and ran.

He heard one of them, Random possibly, shout, "Stop him!" But Danny was beyond reason, running for what little remained of his life. He leaped up the stairs and toward the entrance to the main portion of the bookstore. But even as he reached the top step, Robin stepped into view, and with her—oh, God, Patch was right! With her *was* a demon, the worst demon she could possibly have summoned—

The demon that was his father.

21

Scott and Liz were in the mythology section when they heard the bells over the door tinkle. Scott looked around in time to see a large man with close-cropped iron-gray hair, wearing a black leather trenchcoat, enter the store, followed by a raggedy-looking girl of perhaps fourteen. They moved purposefully toward the stairs to the basement.

"I'll be damned," he said softly.

"Probably," Liz agreed. "Any reason in particular?"

"That big guy in the leather coat—I think it's Edward Thayer. My client."

"You sure?"

"I haven't seen him in twenty years, but yeah—I'm pretty sure."

"What's he doing here?"

"Hell if I know. Damn—looks like this case just got taken away from me. " He started toward the stairs, with her following. He passed a boy wearing dark clothes who loitered near the front of the store.

"YOU'RE GETTING A NICE flow of customers," Craig said to Alice as the door jangle went off again.

"All here for your autographing, no doubt."

He looked around at the overflowing shelves. "Do you ever worry that somebody might steal something?"

Alice smiled, intent on him. "I've always felt that books were a kind of precious thing," she said. "Gateways to other worlds, as it were. If someone wants one so bad that he has to steal it, then I figure that perhaps he should have it."

Craig took her hand in his. "You are quite amazing. I don't think I've ever—"

He was looking around as he spoke, and suddenly he stopped in amazement. That boy standing near the door—he was one of *them*! One of the group he had encountered in the Haight district, the one whose glasses had shown him the vision of Faerie again after all these years.

But what was he doing here?

Even as the question formed in his mind, the boy started toward the stairs, following a couple who had come from the back of the store. Something was going on—Craig had no idea what, but he could *feel* it—a confluence of energy coming together.

Something Alice had just said reverberated in his thoughts. *Gateways to other worlds* . . . could it be?

There was no logic or sense behind it, no earthly reason for the certainty he suddenly felt wash over him, but in that instant, he *knew*. There was a gallitrap near here, perhaps in the store itself! And that boy had come to open it!

"Douglas?"

He felt his knees go abruptly weak. He sat down in the chair behind the desk.

"Douglas, are you all right?" There was real concern in Alice's voice.

"I-I'm fine. Just a touch of dizziness. Nothing to worry about."

Oh, yes, nothing to worry about, old man. Only a second chance, that's all. Another opportunity to rectify, after all these years, the decision that destroyed your life.

"I'll get you some water." Alice bustled off toward the bathroom in the back of the store.

Craig looked around. The boy—the fairy?—had gone downstairs. He stood and started to follow, both hoping and dreading what he might find.

DANNY SKIDDED TO A stop ten feet away from Robin and his father. Behind them he saw Puck come into view.

No, he thought desperately. He turned like a trapped animal and started back down the stairs. He jumped the remaining few steps, knocking over a wire rack of children's books as he lunged down the closest aisle. There was no room in his mind for anything but terror and the panic-ridden desire to escape.

"DANNY!"

Thayer started down the stairs after the boy. He had him now, by God. The girl had been telling the truth. He had to reach Danny before the latter found an exit to the store, if there was one. He hurried down the stairs, the trenchcoat spreading out behind him like black wings.

He passed several more teenagers at the bottom of the stairs. One of them glared at him, then shouted up to the girl, "It won't work, Robin! You're wrong about Danny! He can't do it!"

Thayer brushed past the kid and thundered down the aisle. He didn't know what was going on here, and he didn't care. All that mattered was reaching his son.

"Danny! I won't hurt you! *Danny!*"

DANNY ROUNDED A CORNER, knocking a display dump over with a crash—and found himself facing the wall. There was no way out. His father was right behind him.

"Danny, stop! I just want to talk to you!"

Danny spun and saw his father bearing down on him like a huge black locomotive. He couldn't move—his feet were frozen.

His father grabbed Danny by the shoulders. "Got you! Now you're coming home with me, goddamn it!"

"Let him go," said someone from behind his father.

His father turned, and Danny could see past him down the aisle. Patch stood there, holding a sword that shone with magic, like the light-sabers in *Star Wars*. Danny knew—how, he was not sure—that the sword wasn't real. It was made of glamour, but his father didn't know that.

His father kept a tight grip on Danny's shoulder with one hand while he jammed his other hand into his coat pocket. He pulled out a gun.

Patch laughed. "That won't do you any good, mortal. Lead won't hurt us!"

"Back off, boy, and put down the sword. I don't want to shoot you."

"You don't get it, do you? It won't matter, not unless your bullets are made of iron."

Danny saw his father frown. "Yeah? Well, how about steel, kid? Each bullet has a steel ball bearing in the end."

Patch looked uncertain for a second. Lull stepped out from behind one of the aisles. "Patch, you're going to spoil everything—!"

Patch pushed her away. "You're blind, all of you! You're so desperate to get home that you'll try anything—even threatening one of True Blood! The Seelie Court will know that I was the one who tried to stop you—"

The gun in his father's hand boomed, once, twice, three deafening times. Patch was hurled back against the wall of books. His eyes grew wide, and he dropped the shining sword, which disappeared before it hit the floor. Danny stared, horrified and yet fascinated. There wasn't any blood; instead a silvery fluid trickled between Patch's fingers, smoking and hissing when it hit the floor like water dropped in a fire. The scatterling dropped to his knees, opened his mouth to speak, but instead pitched forward on his face.

"You killed him!" Lull screamed.

Danny's father pointed the gun at her, and she turned and ran.

Patch shimmered, then his body began to fade. For an instant Danny could see the floor right through him. In another second he was no more than a wisp of smoke, and then he vanished altogether.

Danny's father stared in disbelief at the spot on the floor where the scatterling had lain, and said softly, "What the hell is going on here?"

ALICE WAS RETURNING WITH a glass of water when she heard three sharp, loud sounds from the basement, like a car backfiring—or like gunfire. She gasped, dropping the glass, which shattered.

"Douglas? What is happening?"

But Douglas was gone.

SCOTT HEARD THE SHOTS as he and Liz reached the top of the stairs. He stopped, frozen in astonishment. Liz faded

233

back quickly into one of the upper aisles, pulling Scott with her. "Jesus, somebody's got a *gun* down there!" she said.

Scott saw the old woman who owned the store standing next to the door, looking stunned. There was water and broken glass at her feet. She looked around frantically, then saw Scott and Liz.

Scott took Liz by the shoulders and pushed her toward the store's owner. "Get her out of the store," he said.

"Yeah? And what are you going to do?"

Scott took a deep breath and turned toward the stairs. "My job," he said.

DANNY'S FATHER BEGAN TO edge carefully around the area where Patch had fallen, pulling Danny with him. "Come on, Danny. We're getting out of here." His father's face was as gray as his hair, and he was sweating.

Danny tried to pull free of his father's grasp. "No! I don't want to go with you!"

He saw Robin, Puck and the other scatterlings move into view behind his father. His father caught the look and turned. He waved the gun frantically at them. "Get *back!*" he shouted. "Whatever you are, bullets can kill you! If you don't want to die, get the fuck out of here!"

Random, Lull and Pinch looked at each other, then turned and fled toward the stairs, leaving Robin and Puck.

Robin pointed at the gun. "You won't need that," she said. "We won't try to stop you."

At those words, Danny felt as though he had been plunged into a tub of ice. "Robin!" he cried. "Please! You have to help me!"

"She won't help you," his father said. "Who do you think brought me here?"

234

Danny stared at Robin. Her face was a mask. "It's true, Danny," she said. "But if you want to escape, you can. It's simple. Just open the gallitrap."

"I can't!!"

"Yes you can."

"I don't know how!"

"You have to believe in who you are."

His father said, "What're you talking about, girl?" He raised the gun threateningly. "Get out of our way." He started to pull Danny with him.

The fear, the fear he had lived with for so many years, filled him like an electrical current. His father, his own personal demon, had him and there was nothing he could do about it. Nothing . . .

Something.

Deep inside him, at the exact center of his being, he felt it—the same glowing, warming sensation he had felt when Roberto had attacked him. In that instant he realized that *he* had killed Roberto, had been responsible for the barbell magically leaping through the air and striking his friend. He had time for a flash of sorrow and guilt, but that was quickly swept away because he knew, he *knew,* that it was about to happen again.

And he could not stop it.

And he did not want to.

It was the fear that released the power within him. Like a scalpel it lanced through his tortured soul, cut through the lies that had been his entire life, and connected him at last to the power that had always lived within him.

At that moment, he remembered. He knew who he was: a changeling, a scion of the True Blood, a member of the Seelie Court. Why he had been traded at birth for a human child he did not know, nor did it matter at this point.

He knew who he was, and he knew what to do.

Dimly, as though from a far distance, he heard Robin say to Puck, "He sees!"

"Yes. But will he act in time?"

DOUGLAS CRAIG CROUCHED BEHIND a rack of books, watching the scene unfolding before him with horror and amazement. He had seen the man in the leather trenchcoat shoot the boy, had seen the lad dissolve into nothingness. A part of his mind urged him to run, to escape before the gun might be turned on him, but he could no more move than if he had grown roots.

It was going to happen again. He knew it—the gallitrap was going to open again.

And when it did, he would be here.

But—if the gateway to that wondrous land opened now, would he hesitate the same way he had all those years ago? Certainly he had paid the price of admission. But things had changed. As he had feared—and hoped—Alice had awakened something within him that he had thought forever dead. If he had to choose between a new life and a new world, which would he take?

Oh, God, why have you brought me to this place again?

SCOTT MADE HIS WAY carefully down the stairs. Behind him were Liz and Alice—she had introduced herself. Both had insisted on coming with him—Liz because of her devotion to the developing story, and Alice because it was her store.

As they had come down the stairs they had nearly been bowled over by two boys and a girl who had come

236

charging past them and out the front door. It was by far the most prudent course, Scott thought. If he had a lick of sense at all, he would be right behind them.

The three peered around a stack of books. "Jesus Christ," Scott said, his voice a whisper.

Liz and Alice looked over his shoulder at the man in the black leather coat, who was holding on to Danny with one hand and pointing a gun at a boy and a girl. He glanced over at them, saw them.

"You're a day late and a dollar short, Russell," he said. "The case is closed."

DANNY TOOK ADVANTAGE OF his father's distraction to pull himself free. It was easy to do so; he seemed to have a new-found strength. His father reacted in surprise. No; not his father.

"You're not my father," he told him.

Thayer frowned at the conviction in the boy's voice. "That's enough out of you," he said, raising his hand. The gesture would once have sent Danny into spasms of terror. But not now.

The power that had acted before without his conscious will was now his to direct.

Thayer's coat burst into flames.

STILL CONCEALED, DOUGLAS CRAIG watched in amazement as the big man's leather coat suddenly ignited as though by spontaneous combustion. The man screamed in pain and fear. He beat at the flames with his hands, dropping the gun as he did so. He managed to tear himself free of the coat and tossed it away from him. It landed on a nearby stack of paperback books, which ignited in turn.

The three children did not seem unduly surprised or

concerned by this phenomenon. If anything, in fact, the girl seemed pleased.

THAYER STARED IN HORROR at his son—no, not his son, this could never have been his son! The boy had made no move or gesture, but somehow Thayer knew he had been responsible for the fire that had enveloped him. His hands and face were blistered from the heat. And the gun—he had lost the gun . . .

The bookshelf next to him suddenly enkindled with a roar, showering the man with sparks. Thayer screamed again; then, panicked, he turned and ran. Each shelf he passed exploded with a roar as the fire chased him away from the monster he had thought was his son.

"OH, MY GOD!" ALICE cried as the flames leapt toward the ceiling.

Scott saw a fire extinguisher hanging on a nearby wall. He lunged toward it, but already one entire row of books was ablaze. He stumbled back to the others.

"Those kids—where are they?" Liz cried.

"I can't see—smoke's too thick." Scott coughed. He grabbed Liz and Alice, shoved them toward the stairs. "Come on—the whole place is going up!"

"But what about the children?" Alice wailed. "And Douglas—where is he?"

"There's nothing we can do about them! Move it!"

DANNY TURNED TO ROBIN and Puck. He was not afraid anymore, he realized with amazement. He had told himself all his life that there was magic within him, and now, at last, he knew it was true.

"He won't bother us anymore," he said to them.

Robin moved to stand in front of Danny. "I'm sorry for

what I had to do," she said. "You have every right to hate me, my lord."

Danny felt uncomfortable; Robin's attitude toward him had changed somehow, and he wasn't sure why. "I don't hate you," he said. "I think I know why you did what you did. You were just trying to stay alive, same as me."

The flames were all around them now, but somehow, he wasn't worried. He knew there was a way out.

"I'm glad you understand, my lord," Puck said.

"Don't call me that, okay?"

"As you wish," Robin replied. She took his hand and smiled at him. "And now—let's go home, Keymaster."

Danny grinned at her and Puck. As he did so, he opened the gallitrap—it *was* like using a key, only the key was the power inside him. Before them expanded a glowing circle of light, and through it he could see clearly the land he had glimpsed so many times in his dreams— the land in the poster he had kept over his bed, the land where he belonged. The land of Faerie.

"Yes," he said. "Let's go home."

CRAIG TRIED TO STARE through the smoke, his eyes watering. There was a light, a pure golden radiance that was different from the shifting, ruddy hues of the fire. He would have to run in a moment if he was to escape the conflagration—he might already have waited too long. But something about that light—

And then a breeze blew past him, a breeze full of scents that he remembered with every cell of his being. It parted the smoke and he saw the gallitrap, saw it clearly as it opened, saw the empyrean countryside that lay beyond it, and knew what it was.

He watched, transfixed, as the three children walked into the shining light, stepping from linoleum to grass. As

239

they did so, a cat ran across the meadow and leaped past the children, who did not notice it, and through the gallitrap.

The whole place was on fire, Craig realized. There were only two ways out: up the stairs—or through the gallitrap.

He hesitated, torn. Which was it to be?

He heard the cat meowing loudly, confused by the smoke and heat. Poor beast; how had it gotten in there in the first place? He remembered that Alice had had a missing cat.

Craig took two steps toward the gallitrap. It was beginning to close, the ring of light shrinking like it had on that night so long ago. He could still enter it, but—

But what about Alice?

And what kind of man would let a poor cat burn to death?

Craig made his decision. Faerie, no matter how wonderful and magical it might be, was not his world. It never had been. He would be an old man there, an anachronism. He felt grateful; it was not given to many to learn the error of their ways, even this late in life.

Craig turned away from the gallitrap. He snatched up the cat, which promptly dug its claws into his shoulder, and ran through the thickening smoke toward the stairs. As he did so, the light from behind him faded, and the breeze died. He knew the gallitrap had closed again. He felt a single stab of aching loss—and then the smoke closed around him.

SCOTT, LIZ AND ALICE had stopped at the top of the stairs momentarily. They saw the light break through the smoke like the last rays of a sunset penetrating storm

240

clouds. A scent of pure, sweet air dissipated the thick smoke—and they saw the doorway into Faerie.

None of them spoke. They had only a glimpse before the smoke roiled in again and obscured their view. But each saw clearly the three children crossing over into that heavenly land.

Then the smoke billowed up from the blaze, driving them back. *"Douglas!"* Alice cried in despair.

A figure stumbled out of the smoke and up the stairs toward them.

Alice reached forward, grabbed him, pulled him the rest of the way out of the smoke. "Douglas—oh thank God!"

Craig coughed. "Found somebody you might know," he said. He thrust a small dark object toward her. The light from the fire behind him was so intense that she did not know what it was at first. But as she took it in her arms, she knew.

"Mao!"

"Out the door," Scott yelled. *"Now,* or we're dead!"

EDWARD THAYER WAS SURROUNDED by flames. He could feel his hair burning, could feel the skin on his face and neck rising into blister. He couldn't breathe. What had happened, how had it gone wrong? He had been in control, he had found his son . . .

His son . . . yes, it had been Danny, Danny who had done this to him, who had somehow caused the fire. His son. His son had destroyed him.

One of the walls of fire toppled and fell toward him. The last thing he saw was the cover of a burning book as it struck him in the face.

The City Under the Hill.

22

Mao purred against Alice's chest and shoulder as the four of them stood across the street and watched the Looking Glass Bookshop burn. The bright spring day was filled with heat and smoke and sirens and fire trucks spraying water. Firemen aimed hoses that played thick streams of water on the conflagration, but it was useless. They had managed to keep the blaze from spreading to the other buildings, but the store was going to be a total loss. There was quite a bit of her life going up in those flames.

Next to her, Douglas laid a gentle hand on her arm. "Are you all right?"

Alice nodded. "Yes, actually. I'm no doubt a little under-insured, and there are certainly things I'll miss, but things can be replaced. People can't. I'm just glad you got out. Even Mao here is more precious to me than the store." She sighed. "I am sorry about the people who were trapped inside, though."

"No one was trapped there who didn't deserve it," he said. "I saw that man shoot one of the children in cold blood. Anyone who would do that—well, I can't have much sympathy for him. I'll tell you more about it later. You, ah, will come and stay with me, won't you?" He put his arm around her.

She smiled at him. "I'd like that, very much."

DOUGLAS CRAIG STOOD WITH his arm around Alice and thought about what he had seen. The children had been fairies, no doubt—and they had gone home. It had to be true—it *felt* right.

There was only one false note about it. Everything he had read about fairies had indicated that they always left some form of recompense for damage that they caused to good people. Alice was one of the best, without question—and yet they had allowed her store and apartment to burn without attempting to make amends.

Well, it did not really matter. He was by no means a pauper, and Alice would not want for food or shelter. Or even a rebuilt bookstore, if she so desired. What was important was that they were both alive. Alive, and together.

Alice absently scratched the cat's head, then looked down in puzzlement. "Why, Mao, what is this around your neck? Look, Douglas—someone has given Mao a green rhinestone collar."

Craig stared at the cat. Around its neck was a collar of exquisite workmanship. He examined it closely, and as he did so, he started to grin. He had photographed a lot of valuable artifacts in his time, and unless his eyes had gone completely bad, he was certain that the collar Mao wore was of woven gold with settings of filigreed platinum. And those rhinestones were nothing less than eight perfect fingertip-sized emeralds. It was worth enough, he knew, to finance a healthy portion of the rebuilding of the Looking Glass.

As he looked at Alice, and at the crowds of curious bystanders watching the frenetic activity across the street, another feeling stole over Craig: a desire, not for a drink, but for his camera. He wanted to take some pictures.

SCOTT WATCHED THE FIRE as he put the pieces together in his head. There were a few parts of the puzzle he knew he would never find, but all in all, he had enough answers to satisfy himself.

Danny was the key, in more ways than one. The hard case back at the Larkspur had been more right than he knew when he had said that Danny was going back to Fairyland. There *had* been magic in the lad—how or why he had no idea, but it had been enough to open the gallitrap and take himself and the other two with him to that wondrous land. Ed Thayer's charred body was the only one the firemen would find when they went through the ashes—Scott couldn't say he was sorry. He had seen the gun and the terror in Danny's eyes when the boy looked at his father.

The case was over. He didn't have any money, but he had a new confidence in himself. He could do this. What's more, he *liked* doing it. He could probably get a job with another agency, or maybe even start up his own business. After all, what did Travis McGee have that he didn't?

LIZ'S CLOTHES SMELLED OF smoke, her eyes were blood-shot and tearing and her lungs felt like they had been strip-mined, but none of those things mattered. The only thing that mattered was what she had seen. She had witnessed a miracle of the sort that had been sensationalized a thousand times in her paper—people crossing

245

over into another world, a cleaner, purer world. Just knowing it existed somehow made this one look better.

"Looks like you got your story," Scott said.

"Yeah. Too bad I can't use it."

He stared at her. "What?"

"Who'd believe it?"

"Come on. You told me the people who read the *Star* will swallow stranger stuff than this."

Liz smiled. "I know. But those were lies. This was real."

"That makes a difference," he said. It was not a question.

"Damn straight it does. It would be . . . profane, somehow, to dirty this story in that rag I used to work for."

"*Used* to work for?"

Liz grinned at him, feeling the truth of what she was about to say on a cellular level. "I can't go back there. I'm a reporter. It's time I wrote about the truth for a change."

He nodded, grinning at her. The shifting light of the flames reflected from his glasses. Liz shook her head, bemused by what she was saying. "I'm not crazy, am I? There *is* real magic in the world, isn't there?"

"You know there is. We both saw it. Danny Thayer went home."

Liz nodded. "Yeah. And in a way, so have we."

Scott reached out and took her hand in his. They both turned to watch the fire as it flared up to touch the noonday sun.